THE MAKING OF
MR BOLSOVER

Cornelius Medvei

THE MAKING OF MR BOLSOVER

HARVILL SECKER

LONDON

Published by Harvill Secker 2014

2 4 6 8 10 9 7 5 3 1

Copyright © Cornelius Medvei 2014

Cornelius Medvei has asserted his right under the Copyright, Designs and
Patents Act 1988 to be identified as the author of this work

First published in Great Britain in 2014 by
HARVILL SECKER
Random House
20 Vauxhall Bridge Road
London SW1V 2SA

www.vintage-books.co.uk

Addresses for companies within The Random House Group Limited can be found at:
www.randomhouse.co.uk/offices.htm

The Random House Group Limited Reg. No. 954009

A CIP catalogue record for this book is available from the British Library

ISBN 9781846553899 (hardback)

ISBN 9781409041320 (ebook)

The Random House Group Limited supports The Forest Stewardship Council (FSC®), the
leading international forest certification organisation. Our books carrying the FSC label are
printed on FSC® certified paper. FSC is the only forest certification scheme supported by the
leading environmental organisations, including Greenpeace. Our paper procurement policy can
be found at www.randomhouse.co.uk/environment

Mixed Sources
Product group from well-managed
forests and other controlled sources
www.fsc.org Cert no. TT-COC-2139
© 1996 Forest Stewardship Council
FSC

Typeset in Adobe Caslon Pro by Dinah Drazin

Printed and bound in Great Britain by
Clays Ltd St Ives PLC

For my brother and sister

Contents

I

A State of Emergency

There can be few people now who are not familiar with the details of Mr Bolsover's life: his fevered correspondence, his extraordinary political career, his rise and fall, and the time he spent underground. Many of its key moments have passed into folklore, from the note he left on the night he disappeared – '*Gone to join the partisans. Do not try to look for me. P.S. Burn this*' – to the final act in the saga, his betrayal by a former comrade-in-arms. Run to earth by the authorities, he died at last in a hail of bullets, with a shout of defiance on his lips – or alternatively, depending on which account you believe, he slipped through the police cordon and fled to Panama. In view of this, my task is not so much to provide a new record of his life as to fill out and set straight an existing one.

Biographers generally count themselves fortunate to have been able to interview anyone who knew their subject intimately, and in the course of my work I met many such people, newspaper editors, councillors, neighbours and relatives, all of whom were eager to speak to me. It was his nephew Martin Cooper, a local journalist, who warned me that in his experience it was usually the least credible witnesses who were the most forthcoming – an observation which made me uneasy, not least because I had relied on him for much of my testimony. I also had full access to Mr Bolsover's private papers.

It seems to me that political biographies suffer from a tendency to excessive length. Of course, writing a biography of any length is a daunting task – Harold Nicolson, when he began work on his life of George V, noted in his diary that it was 'like starting in a taxi on the way to Vladivostok' – and when a life is painstakingly recorded in several massive volumes, the writer surely deserves credit for a feat of endurance, if nothing else. But there are practical problems with works of this size. A nine-hundred-page hardback is not an easy thing to manage in the bath, and I wonder how many readers have persevered through all eight volumes of the official biography of Winston Churchill, or John Grigg's life of Lloyd George, which was left unfinished at the author's death but still ran to four volumes, or Robert Caro's massive study of Lyndon B. Johnson, about which the *New York Times* recently observed that Caro had now spent longer writing the years of the Johnson presidency than Johnson had spent living them. Then, too, I think that even great lives can be ill-served by a monumental treatment of this kind. The subject is all too often obscured by the mass of detail, and the essence of the person is lost. In contrast, this book is relatively brief, but I do not mean this to diminish in any way the stature of my subject. Plutarch's *Life of Alexander*, after all, runs to fewer than a hundred pages.

The conventional way to begin a biography is at the beginning, with descriptions of the great man in his pram, his first day at school, his first kiss, early days at the biscuit factory, and so on. But I have always suspected that very few readers actually bother with the opening chapters of a biography – particularly a political biography. They turn first to the accounts of political machinations and great affairs of state, the victories and disappointments, the speeches and table talk. Only then, if at all, do they read about his school reports, or the rabbits he kept as a child.

There is also the fact, awkward though it may be for a biographer to acknowledge, that in the lives of most public figures there are long periods in which relatively little happens. Harold Nicolson complained of George V, perhaps an extreme example, that for seventeen years 'he did nothing but kill animals and stick in stamps'. But even the most vigorous and exceptional men and women only function at their full capacity for a relatively short time; their reputations rest on a few remarkable events, and they pass most of their lives in a state of semi-retirement. With this in mind, then, I will pass swiftly over my subject's early years.

The births of great men are traditionally attended by omens and bloody portents. Plutarch tells us that on the night Alexander the Great was conceived, his mother dreamed she had been struck by a thunderbolt, and that on the day of his birth the Temple of Artemis at Ephesus burnt down, while according to the *Secret History of the Mongols* Genghis Khan was born clutching a clot of blood in his fist.

This has not always been the way in our own times. A great man may slip into the world (and, on occasion, leave it as well) unheralded and largely unnoticed, and there was nothing out of the ordinary about the birth of Andrew Lynch on the 16th of October 1958, at the Bromley General Hospital. The birth certificate is nothing to wonder at: delivery normal, weight 7lb 12oz, father a businessman (he ran a furniture showroom), mother a school secretary. The first years of his life were spent within a few miles of his place of birth, in the London suburb of Beckenham, where he lived with his parents and his younger sister, born four years after him.

It is the tranquillity of the suburbs – the well-spaced houses, the quiet tree-lined streets – together with their closeness to the city, that constitutes their appeal to many of their residents. Lynch's parents had spent their whole lives in the outer reaches of south London and showed no sign of wanting to live anywhere else. But it is precisely this combination of factors that fosters in others a desperate urge to escape: the bus leaving for Piccadilly Circus from the end of the road only heightens their sense that real life is going on elsewhere. The explorer Shackleton, who fled Upper Sydenham as soon as he could for the pack ice of the Weddell Sea, is a case in point. As for Lynch, it is true that in 1977, at the age of eighteen, he left home, but he went no further than the University of Leicester, where he studied geography. Here, in his final year, he met his future wife, who was a medical student. After graduation they moved to London, where she qualified as a radiologist and he joined the civil service, working in the Department of Transport. They married in 1984 and bought a small flat in Earlsfield.

As the years passed Mr Lynch grew disenchanted with the civil service. He had been drawn to it at the age of twenty-two, applying for jobs in his final year at university, when it seemed to him a career that he could understand. The idea of serving the public appealed to him, and so did the idea of a secure job, within an organisation that was big enough to offer a variety of experience, and a certain amount of status. It gave him all these things, but gradually he came to believe that the office was an unnatural and constricting habitat for a human being, and the job brought frustrations of its own. Much of his time was spent writing submissions to ministers, who read the submissions, asked for clarification and then failed to implement any of the recommendations. It did not occur to his colleagues to be offended by such behaviour, but Lynch found it vexing when his suggestions were not acted upon. His manager praised the clarity and coherence of his work, but this was no comfort to him.

The civil service in those days set great store by psychological profiling, and after a few months in the department Lynch took a psychometric test with the aim of determining his suitability for a position of responsibility. He scored exceptionally highly for strategic thinking, and for all the qualities deemed necessary in a senior management role: he was an ideal candidate. By his own admission, though, he had very low ratings for the qualities he would need to work his way up, such as deferring to authority and listening to other people's opinions, and he concluded that he had little chance of becoming a permanent secretary. In view of

his later development this strikes me as an uncharac-
teristically defeatist attitude, and perhaps the truth is
that the results of the test provided a justification for his
feelings of disillusionment.

His wife had no such doubts about her choice of
career. She was promoted twice within her unit, and
after a few years started to look around for a more senior post. She wanted to move nearer to her parents,
who lived in Worthing: Lynch did not object to the
idea of leaving London, and she began to apply for jobs
in hospitals on the south coast. When she was offered
a job at the university hospital in Brighton, they sold
their flat in Earlsfield and moved to Lewes, where his
sister lived with her family.

For a few months Mr Lynch continued to commute
to his office, standing every day in the same spot on the
platform, waiting for the train to Victoria, but he was
already looking for another job. He applied for various positions in local government, with little enthusiasm and no success. At last a vacancy came up for a
trainee post in the county library service. The salary was
less than he had been used to, but he did not mind; he
would have an easier journey to work, and his wife at
least was earning a good living. He had always liked
libraries and he thought, irrationally perhaps, that he
would find working in a library more congenial than

an office. Encouraged by his wife, he applied, and got the job.

At weekends they would often drive to the beach at West Wittering, between Portsmouth and Chichester, visiting her parents on the way, and on summer evenings after work they went on shorter excursions nearer to home, to Seaford or to Birling Gap, where the shingle beach was strewn with frilly green sea-lettuce and lumps of chalk, and the sea was always the colour of dishwater. Here his wife would change into her swimming costume and plunge into the waves, while he took off his shoes and socks and paddled for a few minutes before retiring further up the beach to sit with a flask of coffee and a newspaper while he waited for her to come out.

He remained in the library service for eighteen years, working in various branch libraries around the county, in Polegate, Newhaven, and latterly in Uckfield. If his yearly appraisals are anything to go by ('consistently exceeds expectations'), he showed considerable aptitude for the job, and the work must have suited him or he would not have stayed as long as he did.

Despite living in the same town, Martin Cooper had seen little of his aunt and uncle when he was growing up. For many years his aunt had worked irregular hours, and in their free time they kept largely to themselves.

Perhaps if there had been cousins his own age it would have been different. But they had no children.

Around the time that Cooper left school, his aunt was offered a six-month teaching placement at a hospital in New South Wales. As she had been involved for several years in teaching medical students in Brighton, the offer was not unexpected, but her decision to accept it took Mr Lynch by surprise. 'She says she wants a change,' he told Cooper's parents. 'She says she's always wanted to go to Australia. It's the first I've heard of it.'

It was in this period that Cooper first got to know his uncle. Worried perhaps that he might be lonely, Cooper's parents invited him round once a week for dinner, and Cooper found him stimulating company. His parents' mealtime conversations were centred on the same few familiar and uncontroversial subjects, such as garden planting schemes and cookery, which they continued after twenty-two years of marriage to find deeply absorbing, and Cooper welcomed the new note introduced by his uncle, with his combative manner and his readiness to turn any conversation into a debate.

One Saturday morning he appeared at Cooper's parents' house unannounced, and asked if Cooper wanted to go for a walk. He cut an arresting figure as he stood there on the doorstep, rocking back and forth on his heels. He had a long scarf wrapped round his neck and tucked into the front of his jacket, which made his chest bulge like a turkey's. On his feet he had a pair of old rain-stained brogues with the colour leached out of them, and he was wearing a pair of pale yellow cord trousers which were slightly too short and revealed his ankles. His shirt was tucked in and his hair was tidy, but he still appeared dishevelled. There was an air of dislocation about him, as if he had just got off a ship after a long voyage and hadn't yet found his land legs.

Cooper had been going to help his father clear the gutters behind the house, and then to have his hair cut, but he decided that both could wait. He fetched his coat and shut the door behind him, and followed his uncle down the street. They crossed the main road and were soon climbing the narrow path up the flank of Malling Down, above the allotment gardens.

Mr Lynch had the restless energy that drives chief executives and captains of industry to swim a mile every morning before breakfast, or to hurl themselves down the ski slopes – an energy which must be harnessed or wear the individual into a decline. Gladstone had it and worked it off by chopping vast quantities of firewood, while Churchill occupied himself by building walls on his estate. Lynch preferred to climb hills, the steeper the better. That morning he was filled with an almost superhuman vigour. He strode up the steep hillside, talking constantly, while Cooper hurried after him gasping for breath. At last, on the windy heights of Cliffe Hill, where the shadows of clouds raced across the close-cropped grass, he paused in the lee of a thorn bush to contemplate the view spread out below: the loops of the River Ouse gleaming in the sun, the stump of the castle rising above the rooftops, the white gash of the chalk pit on Offham Hill away to the right, and the rooks in the foreground, tumbling in the wind like scraps of burnt paper.

'The wind blows on the great man and the small man alike,' he told Cooper. 'But the great man bends in the wind like grass, and the small man breaks.'

Cooper understood then that exercise was not the only purpose of this breathless walk. Mr Lynch was the kind of person who craved a setting for his conversations, feeling the mundane surroundings of the home or the local pub inadequate and requiring a backdrop more in keeping with his sense of drama.

Fortunately Lewes is well supplied with dramatic settings. The following weekend they walked along the high muddy banks of the Ouse, out across the marshes and back. Cooper had learnt from the experience of their first outing, and this time he brought a notepad and a pencil, so that when he was really out of breath he would have an excuse to stop and fish them out of his pocket and make a few hasty notes. His uncle stood still then for a few moments, but the note-taking only encouraged him – the flow of talk became faster, his gestures wilder and more animated, and as they resumed their walk the passers-by would look at him askance and back out of the way.

They rested that afternoon on a bench below the flint wall of the Bowls Club, overlooking Convent Field and the football pitches, and sheltered from the wind by the brick buttresses against which generations of dogs had cocked their legs. It was here that Mr Lynch made the remark which Cooper took down in his notebook: 'What the small man looks for in others the great man looks for in himself.'

In those days Cooper had not yet resolved the question of whether his uncle was a great man or a small man.

It is always tempting for the biographer to dramatise the role of chance. As the task of biography is to provide order and explanations, to impose narrative on the course of events, this temptation is natural. Examining a life with the benefit of hindsight, it is easy to look at any unlikely occurrence – a brush with death, an unexpected meeting – and see the hand of destiny at work.

But I think it is more honest to admit that even great men are subject to twists of fate, and to agree with whoever it was who observed that destiny is nothing more than chance observed in the rear-view mirror.

A month or two after his wife went away, Mr Lynch was at the issue desk in the library one afternoon – it must have been a Tuesday, because according to the rota he was only on duty at the issue desk on Monday and Thursday mornings and Tuesday afternoons – when he was called by a colleague to help in a dispute with a borrower over a fine. He went over to see what was happening, whereupon, in the words of the official report on the incident, 'a violent assault took place'.

Lynch always maintained afterwards that he had been hit over the head with a book (Tressell's *The Ragged Trousered Philanthropists*, eight weeks overdue, which in its hardback edition would have floored an ox). But the report makes no mention of this. Neither of his colleagues who were there at the time could remember the title of the book, and they gave differing accounts of what happened. One told me that Mr Lynch had been assaulted with a book, but that it had been thrown at him across the desk. According to her colleague, however, the borrower had put the book down on the desk, then leant across and punched him in the stomach, before turning round and walking calmly out of the building.

As all the accounts are contradictory, I see no real reason not to accept Lynch's version of events, and to recognise his experience as one that sits in the long tradition of physical shocks leading to flashes of insight, like that experienced by Archimedes getting into his bath, or Newton under the apple tree. I concluded that it was psychologically necessary for him to believe in the violent blow to the head, followed by a sudden illumination, as a way of accounting for the dramatic changes in his life that followed.

In any case, the immediate outcome is not in doubt: his colleagues helped him to his feet, someone went to get some ice, someone else made him a cup of tea with four sugars, and the library manager told him to take the rest of the afternoon off. 'And once I got outside,' he said afterwards, 'I realised I never wanted to go back.'

It was easily arranged. He was examined by a doctor, who told him to take a week off work to recover from his injuries. At the end of the week he went to see the doctor again and was pronounced unfit to return to work. The physical injuries were healing well, the doctor said, but the psychological damage was more serious. The council gave him six months' sick leave, on full pay. They probably felt they had got off lightly; he might have sued them for failing to prevent the assault.

I have not been able to establish exactly how badly

the incident really affected Lynch's health, but he took immediately to his new life of ease. In the first weeks of his sick leave he was full of barely suppressed excitement, like a schoolboy at the beginning of the holidays. He still woke at the same time on weekday mornings and would get up, dress in some old clothes and go out for a long and leisurely walk round the streets of the town just as everybody else was hurrying to work.

For Mr Lynch this was of course a time of recuperation and adjustment to his new circumstances, but I think too that in retrospect these weeks of apparent idleness may be viewed as a crucial stage in his development, like the months the young Gladstone spent in Italy before his first entry into Parliament in 1832, a period of lying fallow, marshalling his resources, gathering strength for the struggles that lay ahead. If the weather was fine he liked to sunbathe in his swimming trunks on the small patch of lawn in front of his house until he was deep brown and wrinkly all over, and then he would put some clothes on and get out his bicycle and ride out to one of the nearby villages, to Laughton or to East Chiltington where there was a pub that he particularly liked.

On wet days he haunted the second-hand bookshops, the junk shops in Cliffe High Street, and most of all the Antiques Centre in the converted church on Station Street, where the price tickets attached to long-case clocks and glass lampshades fluttered in the blast from the fan heater. Here it was always warm and brightly lit, and he could browse for hours among the cabinets of old china, the drawers full of silver-plated cutlery, the backgammon sets and enamel dishes and back issues of *Military Modelling* magazine and antique gardening tools, exchanging a friendly word with the other browsers who shuffled up and down the narrow aisles, picking up objects and examining them through their reading glasses, happily hunting for non-existent bargains, watched by sharp-eyed old ladies who sat at the counters drinking endless cups of milky tea.

His excursions with his nephew continued alongside these solitary outings. One stifling summer night Cooper was about to go to bed when he received a telephone call from Mr Lynch.

'Hot enough for you?' he asked. 'How about a swim?'

'Will the pool be open at this time of night?' Cooper asked.

'Almost certainly not.'

'Then where …?'

'Listen,' his uncle said, 'I don't have time to explain now. Just meet me in front of St John's Church in twenty minutes. And bring a towel.'

The bricks and the tarmac still held the warmth of the

day as Cooper made his way through the town centre. The backstreets were dark and empty, the pavements were sticky under the lime trees and the shouts of the people leaving the pubs sounded thin and listless in the heat. The dry grass on the hilltops shone like snow in the moonlight. As he came down Abinger Place towards the church, the familiar figure of his uncle stepped from behind the elder bush on the corner.

'Nothing like a midnight swim for cooling off,' he remarked as they went down the hill and along the path that led to the open-air pool. The ducks on Pells Brook quacked and splashed in the darkness and there was a smell of waterweed in the air as Mr Lynch clambered over the gate. After a brief hesitation, Cooper followed him.

Leaving their clothes under a bench, they pulled back the cover and slipped into the water. As they swam towards the deep end the rounded summit of Malling Hill came into view above the roofs of the industrial estate, and when they turned and swam back the other way they could see the moon shining through the branches of the pine trees that grew behind the changing rooms. But it was Mr Lynch who drew Cooper's attention. He propelled himself through the water with a jerky but vigorous breaststroke, breathing hard through his nose, with his head straining clear of the surface.

It surprised me that Cooper should have embarked so readily on this and other transgressions. By his own account he had been a model student at school, if not a brilliant one, and I wondered whether he had been making up for a lack of schoolboy escapades. But when I asked him he insisted that this was not the case. He had felt at the time, he said, as though his uncle was sounding him out for some future role, that this was a test of character that he must not fail.

The week after their swimming excursion, Cooper got his first inkling of what that future role might be when he accompanied his uncle to a sale at one of the local auction rooms. In the yard outside they joined the drifting throng of people who were poking about and examining the lots, purposefully opening and shutting the lids of chests and trunks, measuring the height of wardrobes, scribbling in notepads, eating toffees and sucking at the ends of roll-up cigarettes. A few wailing toddlers stumbled after their parents among the chairs and table legs, and Cooper saw an old man breaking off a conversation with his neighbour to bang his stick experimentally against a tin bath.

'Seen anything you like the look of?' his uncle asked after a while.

'Not really.'

'There must be something.' He leafed through his catalogue. 'How about this – lot ninety-seven. Approximately three hundred bouncy balls. Estimate five to eight pounds.'

'What am I going to do with three hundred bouncy balls?'

'It's a good price. Think how much they'd cost if you wanted to buy them individually.'

Cooper was about to ask if there was anything his uncle wanted to buy himself, when a man in a frayed straw hat came up behind them and clutched at Mr Lynch's shoulder.

'This is the place to be, isn't it?' he said. 'I'm going to bid on a 1950s croquet set – full size!' He shook their hands and disappeared into the saleroom.

'He's here every week,' said Mr Lynch dismissively, 'he never buys anything.'

He glanced up at the sky, which was dark and overcast. 'Looks like rain,' he said. 'Let's go inside while we can still find a seat.'

The saleroom was the size of a barn, but it felt cluttered all the same. Chests of drawers and drinks cabinets and grandfather clocks had been pushed up against the walls, with mirrors and pictures hanging above them. Behind the auctioneer's desk there were long trestle tables and metal shelves crammed with more items:

boxes of books and china, silver-plated teapots, a row of paraffin lamps.

'You could pick up a whole lifetime's worth of junk here if you wanted it,' Mr Lynch observed. 'Get rid of it as well. And who knows where all these things will be tomorrow?'

There was no designated seating. Instead the bidders had made themselves comfortable on the armchairs and sofas which were lots in that afternoon's furniture sale, and which had been drawn up in rows facing the auctioneer's desk. Near the back of the room Cooper spotted a sofa that was still free, and they hurried to sit down on it.

The sale was already under way, the auctioneer keeping up his baffling hypnotic patter while his assistant moved round the room pointing out the lots.

'Fifty-two. Victorian kitchen chairs. Nice little pair of chairs for twenty pounds. A tenner. Take five. Five's bid, take six. Eight. Eight pounds the chairs, who's ten? Ten I've got, take twelve? Going ten, we'll sell away at ten.'

Cooper's first impression was that the auctioneer was carrying on this performance purely for their entertainment. It was some time before he managed to spot the brief nods and the raised fingers which indicated that bids were being made.

'Sixty-eight is the dressing table with mirror.'

'This is the one!' Mr Lynch whispered.

'What do you need a dressing table for?'

'Sh.'

'We start in at thirty-five, take eight. Thirty-five pounds bid, eight I'll take. Thirty-eight I have, forty is there? Forty, thank you. Forty with me, any advance? All good and done at forty.'

'Forty pounds?' Lynch muttered indignantly. 'It's worth more than that. It's solid mahogany.'

'You're selling your dressing table?'

'It's not mine, it's your aunt's.'

'Why are you selling it?'

'I don't need a dressing table, do I? There's a mirror in the bathroom.'

'But won't she want it when she gets back?'

The auctioneer was calling out the next lot, and Lynch did not answer straight away. He did not seem to have heard the question. Then with a great creaking of the sofa springs he turned to Cooper.

'They've offered to extend her placement for another six months,' he said. 'Between you and me, I don't think she's coming back.'

'Seventy-two. Box of Denby ware. All the Denby there, various patterns. Thirty-five pounds to start me...'

'I'd have gone to Australia if she'd wanted me to,' said Mr Lynch. 'I'd have gone anywhere.' His face was haggard. 'It's not exactly a surprise,' he said, 'but I didn't expect it to happen like this.

'I don't have a bad word to say about her,' he added. 'She's a very capable woman, very level-headed.'

It occurred to Cooper afterwards that Lynch's comments were not so much an assessment of his wife's character as an explanation of why she had left him.

In those days Cooper had just started working as a junior reporter on the *Sussex Journal* and he was, by his own admission, an unusually callow nineteen-year-old with very little conversation and no experience of the world. In view of this, it is perhaps surprising that Lynch should have sought him out in this way. But the appeal of a willing and more or less sympathetic listener should not be underestimated, and the fact is that in those days, after Lynch's wife went away, there were not many people he could talk to. Like many middle-aged men, he had numerous acquaintances but few close friends. There were in fact only two; one was a friend from his youth, now a quantity surveyor in Torbay, and the other was a former colleague by the name of Rawlings, who had joined the civil service at the same time as him and remained there, attaining some dizzy height in the Department of Health. Rawlings had two teenaged children and lived in Leighton Buzzard, commuting every day to Euston; they kept in touch in a perfunctory way, but seldom saw each other.

Mr Lynch was not starved of company; he got on well with his neighbours, and he often met his former colleagues for a drink in the evenings. But that was not the same as having a regular listener, a confidant, someone to whom you could describe your ideas at length, with whom you could return to a topic again and again and expand on it. From this point of view his nephew was ideal. In his dealings with me Cooper adopted the persona of a hard-bitten reporter. But I could imagine him at nineteen, awkward and impressionable, hanging on his uncle's every word. They also had this in common, that despite the difference in their ages, they were at a similar stage in their lives. Lynch's wife no longer needed him. His employers had found him eminently replaceable. At the age of fifty-four he was, like his nephew, seeking a place in the world, and also an identity. He was about to find both.

But despite their rapidly developing bond, Cooper still found that there were gulfs in understanding between them. One fine clear night his uncle took him to the top of Mount Harry, one of the hills on the west side of Lewes, to look at the night sky. From this vantage point they could see the lights of the farms and villages below them stretching away towards the Weald, and the orange glow of Brighton and Rottingdean behind the hills to the south. The ground fell away on all sides, and it seemed to Cooper that they were on a small island of tussocky grass and gorse bushes, detached from the rest of the landscape. The illusion was strengthened by the wind in the trees further down the hillside, which sounded like waves breaking on a beach.

The sheep which had gathered round them as they made their way to the hilltop moved away and could be heard cropping busily at the grass as Mr Lynch set up his astronomical telescope and spread a rug on the ground for them to sit on. From further away came the cry of an owl, and the whine and rumble of an airliner on its approach to Gatwick. Above their heads the sky was black and thickly frosted with stars. They took it in turns to peer into the eyepiece while Mr Lynch pointed out the craters on the moon and the cloud-belts of Jupiter. Then he took a flask out of his briefcase and poured them both a cup of coffee while he trained the telescope on the shipping in the Channel, which was visible through a gap in the downs behind Newhaven.

'The world is shrinking,' he told Cooper. 'There are twice as many people in it as there were when I was born. Vast populations are on the move. That's one of the busiest shipping lanes in the world down there. Where does a man go now when he wants to get away?'

Cooper had no answer to this question, and he did not know whether one was expected. Talking to his parents he always knew where he was, but conversations with his uncle were punctuated by moments like this when, swept along by the flow of talk, he would suddenly find himself out of his depth.

Mr Lynch did not provide an answer on that occasion, but he must have gone on thinking about it, because going through his papers I came across the following essay, written about this time, in which he takes up the theme at length:

In the Manor Gardens in Eastbourne there is a small but striking building, a tall, eight-sided structure on a stone plinth, with latticework windows and a thatched roof topped off with a wooden spike. It is known as the Hermitage, and it was built for an occupant of the Manor towards the end of the eighteenth century, when there was something of a vogue for hermits among the English gentry. All over the country, landowners were building grottoes and thatched huts in secluded corners of their estates and looking for suitably picturesque and dishevelled candidates to inhabit them. William Kent built a hermitage at Kew for Queen Caroline, and Jonathan Swift wrote an epigram about it. At Painshill Park in Surrey, the seat of the Hon. Charles Hamilton, the resident hermit lasted no more than a few weeks before decamping to a nearby inn. Gilbert White, the naturalist and rector of Selborne in Hampshire, held dinner parties at which his brother Henry appeared dressed as a hermit to entertain the guests.

But this was by no means a new obsession. The figure of the hermit has held a fascination both for the general public and for those in positions of power at least since the days of the early Church, when Simeon the Stylite preached from his pillar to mass audiences and exchanged letters with the Byzantine emperor Theodosius II. The house built by Louis XV at Fontainebleau for his mistress Madame de Pompadour was known as the Hermitage, and Catherine the Great gave the same name to her private apartments in the Winter Palace. Although there may be less interest in hermits nowadays, it seems to me that the hermit offers a cure for a particularly contemporary anxiety, which might be termed a lack of *alternative space*.

For most of human history there has been somewhere else to go. There were always places close at hand, deserts and forests and mountain ranges where authority could be evaded or unfashionable virtues cultivated or new forms of social order experimented with. It was also possible to set out in search of new lands altogether, as the Vikings did, and the Polynesian voyagers in their outrigger canoes. Later there was the idea of the New World, which drew everyone from the *Mayflower* pilgrims to Coleridge and Southey, with their plan for a Pantisocracy on the banks of the Susquehanna.

It is only comparatively recently that this kind of alternative existence has ceased to be possible, but the impulse to withdraw from social life remains. It is telling that the exploits of round-the-world yachtsmen and polar explorers captured the popular imagination at about the time when the opportunity to withdraw was no longer available to the general public.

How then in the present day can this enduring human impulse be catered for? I am not convinced that the experiences of solitary adventurers are of any practical value to the man in the street, and as for more philosophical lessons, perhaps it is wrong to expect anything of the kind: such people are too physically drained by the practicalities of day-to-day survival, too preoccupied with the routines necessary to preserve their sanity during long periods of isolation. A case in point is Francis Chichester's account of his solo circumnavigation, *Gipsy Moth Circles the World*. In it, Chichester provides an exhaustive inventory of his stores, so that the reader knows exactly what kind of biscuits he had with him when he rounded the Horn (fourteen packets of ginger nuts, four packets of chocolate and twelve of plain digestives). He shares his views on diet – 'I attach enormous importance to garlic' – and laments the loss overboard of his best screwdriver. But anyone looking for deeper thoughts will be disappointed.

And so I come back to the figure of the hermit, and in particular the stylite. To the hagiographers, the stylite's pillar represented a wish to escape the sordid clutches of a sinful world. To Gibbon, whose hostility to the early Christian ascetics is well documented, it was a stage on which the ragged exhibitionists could display themselves more effectively to the credulous masses. But another interpretation is possible. Most of the stylites established themselves in relatively secluded places, near churches or monasteries. A few, though, set up their pillars within the city walls, in public squares or marketplaces, and in doing so, I think, they demonstrated a true understanding of the stylite's purpose. This was above all to achieve a change of perspective, both literal and metaphorical – to withdraw from society while remaining present, to be in it but not of it. Thoreau had a similar goal in mind when he went to live by Walden Pond. 'The Concord nights,' he once wrote, 'are stranger than the Arabian nights.'

Despite his withdrawal from society, there was a social dimension to the life of the hermit. People credited him with wisdom, wanted to believe that he had all the answers, and went to him for advice on everything from their love lives to political conundrums. Gibbon saw this as evidence of the hermit's hypocrisy, courting society when he claimed to be a recluse. But it is surely possible that Gibbon was wrong, that the hermit was not a posturing charlatan, and that in fact his peculiar viewpoint gave him valuable insights which were not accessible to anyone else.

The hermit might also function as a counterweight to the rest of society. I picture a hermit not just in the Manor Gardens in Eastbourne, but in every borough and local authority, and a stylite in every office tower in the City, with living quarters forty floors up, resting on a pallet stuffed with shredded documents, riding up and down in the lifts, patrolling the windswept plazas of Canary Wharf, engaging the harried office workers in discussions of Truth and Eternity in the manner of William Blake, and sitting in on meetings of the board. A small counterweight, admittedly, but as the law of the lever states, if the beam is long enough, then the exertion of a relatively small force can shift a considerable mass. 'Give me a place to stand,' said Archimedes, 'and I will move the earth.'

2

A Change of Address

Mr Lynch was not a man of extravagant tastes. His outgoings had always been modest, and by visiting his sister's house on Sunday and Wednesday evenings for meals he was able to reduce his expenses yet further. But even modest expenses cannot be met without some kind of income; Lynch had none, his savings would be spent sooner or later, and it would be several years before he could draw his pension.

A little hardship in the early stages of a political career is not necessarily a bad thing. Tales of triumph over adversity are always popular with the public, and political leaders of all stripes have found themselves looking back with nostalgia, from the comfort of their official residence, on a youth spent herding goats or starving in the Vienna cafés. But Mr Lynch was perhaps unaware as yet that he had embarked on a political career, and meanwhile the problem of funding remained.

He was less fortunate in this regard than many pro-fessional revolutionaries. There were no well-wishers to give him donations. He could not tour the United States as Castro had done, soliciting contributions from wealthy American sympathisers. No one would hire him for speaking engagements or lecture tours, and unlike Trotsky he could not fall back on the serial publication of his memoirs in the *Saturday Evening Post*.

For some time, though, he seemed oblivious to these financial imperatives; at least, he never spoke of them to Cooper, and appeared preoccupied with other projects, like his programme of country walks. He generally took a camping stove and a kettle with him, and he kept an eye out for sheltered places where he could brew up. One favourite spot was up on Malling Down, in a clearing among the thorn bushes, well out of the wind, where the turf was springy and comfortable and he had a bird's-eye view of the town below. But as he roamed further afield he soon gravitated towards a small wood on the edge of the marshes between Lewes and Barcombe. Here there was a sunny and secluded glade carpeted with dog's mercury and bluebells where he would recline on the blanket he had brought, watching the flies as they tacked about in the shafts of sunlight that came through the canopy and listening to the birds singing and the sound of the wind in the branches above his head. If the weather was warm he would take off his shoes and socks and sit with his feet in the stream that ran through the middle of the wood. One day, inspired perhaps by a wish to make his mark on the landscape, or perhaps by some primitive burrowing instinct, he brought a spade from home and dug himself a hole. This was intended to provide shelter from the wind that blew up the valley from the sea, and also to shield him from the curious eyes of the children who lived in the nearby houses and often played in the wood: he hardly ever saw them, but he had found their discarded crisp packets and inspected the bivouacs they had built from fallen branches.

In the bottom of this hole he put a layer of spruce twigs and on windy days he would spread the blanket on top of the twigs and stretch out on his back, looking up into the canopy of leaves. Later he roofed over the foxhole with a piece of corrugated iron, which he concealed by scattering it with earth and leaf litter. This allowed him to leave the blanket and tea things in the hole overnight, so that he did not need to carry them with him every time he went out there.

But it was not long before his tranquillity was disturbed. The first Cooper knew of it was when he answered the door at his parents' house one Wednesday evening to find his uncle standing on the step with his blanket over his arm.

'You're early,' Cooper said.

'I know.'

The blanket was wet through and, Cooper noticed when he looked down, so were his uncle's shoes. 'I didn't realise it had been raining,' he said.

'It hasn't. This was an act of sabotage. Can I come in? I want to use the tumble dryer.'

He put his blanket and socks in the dryer and borrowed a pair of boots – Mr Lynch took a size ten, the same as Cooper's father – and they went out to the wood, where Cooper saw for himself what had happened. Somebody had built a dam across the stream, diverting the flow of water into the clearing so that it flooded Mr Lynch's dugout. Then the dam had been breached and the water had resumed its regular course. The ground in the clearing was sodden underfoot, and the dugout itself full of water. The remains of the dam could still be seen, an untidy structure of branches and rocks incorporating the piece of corrugated iron that Lynch had used as a roof.

'Do you know who did it?'

'Some children,' his uncle said. 'I don't know their names. It was a territorial dispute.'

So far Cooper's parents had not paid much attention

to Lynch's activities. But since he was eating at their table and using their tumble dryer, they no doubt felt they had earned the right to mock him a little.

'You should get yourself a pair of wellington boots,' said Cooper's mother.

'Try a tree house next time,' Cooper's father suggested. 'You won't get flooded in a tree house.'

Mr Lynch appeared untroubled by these barbs, which he perhaps saw as evidence of his relatives' small-mindedness, or as confirmation of the truth that the prophet is without honour in his own country. There was in any case a distinctly defensive air to their taunts. Sitting there in the kitchen with Cooper's father's slippers on his feet, he did not look very threatening, but a middle-aged rebel is in some ways more subversive and dangerous than a young one, and Cooper's parents must have sensed this. If Cooper had been the one rebelling, they might have been more indulgent. But for Mr Lynch, after years of departmental meetings and wedding anniversaries and mortgage repayments, suddenly to leave it all behind and take to the woods – this was a genuine outrage.

Cooper did not share his parents' attitude. He was determined not to join in their mockery, and when he asked his uncle what he planned to do next it was in a suitably respectful tone of voice.

'Never mind my plans,' said Mr Lynch with such asperity that Cooper was taken aback. 'I'm more concerned about you.'

'What do you mean?'

'You've got to get your life in some kind of order. All right, so you're going to be a journalist, that's terrific. But what are you doing still living with your parents, at your age? How old are you, by the way?'

'Nineteen.'

'Nineteen already,' he said. 'It's not natural. A healthy young man like you, with a steady job, earning a living – don't you think it's time you had a place of your own?'

'I like living here,' Cooper said.

'Maybe you do, but what do your parents think?' Cooper's parents were watching this exchange with bemusement from the other side of the table. 'You should consider them too, you know. When are you going to get out from under their feet? This isn't a big house, after all – I'm sure they could use the space.'

'What are you trying to say?' Cooper's mother asked.

'Do you want to rent my house?'

Cooper did not reply straight away. He had never doubted that his uncle was an intelligent man, but this was the first intimation he had had of Mr Lynch's extraordinary capacity for strategic thinking. It was a brilliant stroke, all the more dumbfounding for being so unexpected. All this time, when he had seemed unwilling or unable to confront the reality of his financial situation, inclined to waste his energy on diversions, some deeper level of his mind had been preparing a solution.

'But where are you going to live?' said Cooper.

'Oh, there's a place I've got my eye on.'

'Is it in Lewes?'

'Just outside. You'll have to come and see it when I've settled in.'

Cooper decided to accept his uncle's offer. He was in no particular hurry to get away from his parents, but he liked the idea of having a place of his own. Besides, his uncle's house was closer to the newspaper office than his parents', and the walk to work would only take him a few minutes.

Barcombe Crescent stood on the very edge of the town, where the gardens backed onto the open downland. Mr Lynch's house, number seventeen, was one end of a terrace, with a pyracantha growing by the door and a bumpy lawn that ran down to the pavement. Cooper went round a few days later, so that his uncle could show him how to work the heating and hot water and hand over a set of keys. The rent was to be paid monthly, in advance, by bank transfer.

It was the first time Cooper had been to the house since his aunt had gone away, but very little had changed. The only signs of his aunt's absence were the marks left in the bedroom carpet where her dressing table had been and the layer of dust on all the surfaces, something that she would never have allowed.

'Won't you be taking any of the furniture with you?' he asked.

'No.'

'So the place you're moving to,' Cooper said, 'it's furnished already?'

'More or less.'

Cooper moved in that weekend. After breakfast on Saturday morning he walked across the town carrying a large rucksack which contained his clothes and washing things. He had also packed a few boxes, which his parents brought over later in their car. As he walked along Barcombe Crescent he could hear unseen sparrows cheeping in the privet hedges, and from a back garden came the smell of burning rubbish. There was no one about except a postman, somebody tinkering under the bonnet of a van, and a cat which caught sight of him and bolted back inside.

From the driveway Cooper could look down across the roofs of the houses on the other side of the street and see the trampolines and sheds and lilac bushes in the steep back gardens, and beyond them more roofs and rows of parked cars, all the way down the hill to the centre of the town. He stood at the door trying the keys one after another until he found the right one. He turned on the hot water, then went upstairs to unpack. The bedroom cupboards were full of clothes, suits and shirts on hangers, and a few pairs of shoes belonging to his aunt, but the chest of drawers was empty, and he unpacked his clothes and put them in the drawers. Then he stuffed the empty rucksack under the bed and took his washing things into the bathroom. After that he found a towel in the airing cupboard and put sheets on the bed.

It was not long before Cooper met his neighbours. There was an elderly couple on one side, the Pritchards, who spent a lot of time in their garden, which they kept extremely tidy, and on the other a woman of about fifty who introduced herself as Annie Hazelhurst. She was the owner of the cat. They were all sorry to hear that Mr Lynch had moved out. He had been a good neighbour, Miss Hazelhurst said, very quiet and considerate, and they had had some long talks across the fence, especially after his wife went away. The Pritchards agreed, adding that he always took his bins in, he didn't leave them out on the pavement like some people did.

'And you,' said Mrs Pritchard, 'you're a lucky young man to have a house to yourself.'

'I expect he'll be having lots of parties,' her husband said. 'I know I would have done, at your age.'

But he was wrong. Cooper's life at Barcombe Crescent, as he described it to me, was one of blameless respectability. On weekday mornings he would get up shortly before eight, have a shower and iron a shirt. After a quick breakfast of coffee and toast he would leave the house and walk down the hill and into town. The newspaper office in those days was at the far end of the High Street, and after work he would stop off at the shops to buy groceries on his way home. In the evenings after dinner he might watch television in the front room or sit outside the back door with a bottle of beer. At weekends he worked in the garden. He cut the grass and hacked back the undergrowth behind the house and dug over a small piece of ground near the kitchen door for a vegetable bed. One evening he saw a hedgehog on the lawn, and after that he would sometimes put a saucer of cat food out for it on the back step.

I listened to all this with mounting impatience. It was not just the banality of Cooper's recollections that irritated me. Any biographer would have jumped at the opportunity to see the subject's house exactly as it was when he left it, and not just to visit, not to be shown round, but actually to live there for an extended period, as Cooper had done – to eat off his plates, to finger his books, to answer his telephone, to doze in his favourite chair. Even Boswell, 'a man without delicacy, without shame', as Macaulay describes him, never got the chance to sleep in Dr Johnson's bed. My irritation was unfair: Cooper never set himself up as a biographer. All the same, I had the sense of an opportunity missed.

Both Mr Lynch's whereabouts and his activities during the period that followed remain obscure. He had not provided a forwarding address, or arranged for his mail to be redirected. Instead, when Cooper arrived on that first Saturday morning, he found that his uncle had left a note instructing him to leave any letters on a shelf in the tool shed at the side of the house, from where he would collect them at his own convenience. Cooper guessed that Mr Lynch had not given him these instructions during their earlier meeting at the house because he did not want to answer questions on the subject of his new living arrangements. Now, of course, Cooper was more curious than ever, but he imagined that sooner or later they would meet and everything would be explained.

As it turned out, he did see Mr Lynch shortly after his move, but the circumstances of their encounter did nothing to dispel the mystery. It was a Saturday afternoon, and he was returning from London on the train. On the stretch of line between Cooksbridge and Lewes the train slowed as it entered a cutting with sandy banks, pockmarked by rabbit holes, where Cooper had often seen foxes sunning themselves. This time when he looked out of the window there were no foxes to be seen, but halfway up the bank he caught sight of his uncle, crouching motionless in a patch of rosebay willowherb. The thin stems provided limited cover, but he made no effort to conceal himself. Cooper had no idea what he was doing there. He did not appear to be watching the train; it was as if its passing had interrupted him in some other activity, like the rabbits further along the cutting, which stopped nibbling the grass and sat up when the train went by. He could only have got there by climbing the fence at the top of the bank – there were a number of overgrown places where he could have done this unobserved – or by cutting the wire. If nothing else, he was trespassing on the railway, and there was no shortage of notices on the station platforms and at the level-crossing gates to remind him that this offence carried a fine of up to a thousand pounds. But at this time in the afternoon, travelling in this direction, the train was almost empty, and glancing around his carriage Cooper saw that the other passengers were otherwise occupied: a mother jiggling her baby to keep it from crying, a girl shouting excitedly into her phone and an old man dozing in a corner seat.

Not long after this initial sighting, Cooper was walking up the path by St Anne's Church one morning on his way to work when he saw a figure some distance ahead of him, scrambling over the flint wall of the cemetery. He was carrying a bundle, which he rested on the wall as he climbed down into the street. As he hoisted the bundle onto his back again he coughed, and Cooper knew for certain that it was his uncle. He hurried away up the road, too far ahead for Cooper to catch him without breaking into a run, and disappeared round a corner.

When Cooper drew level with the place where his uncle had emerged, he stopped and looked over the wall. The grass was long and the cow parsley was in flower, reaching almost to the top of the gravestones. There was a trampled patch just behind the wall where Lynch had climbed over, and in the grass beyond it a faint line of tracks could be made out. But as to what he had been doing there, whether he had been gathering simples or sleeping rough, Cooper was none the wiser.

Nevertheless, he was concerned. There was no answer when he called Mr Lynch's mobile phone, but he had noticed that the post was being collected from the shelf in the shed at regular intervals, and he decided to write his uncle a note, asking if everything was all right. When he looked in the shed a day later the note was still there, but the morning after that it had gone, and when he left the office that evening he found his uncle waiting outside. He was sitting on the railing by the entrance, where the newspaper staff chained their bicycles.

'Busy day?' he asked.

'What are you doing here?'

'I got your message,' he said. 'I thought you might like to see my new place.'

It had been a tiring day, and Cooper had been looking forward to going home, but he did not hesitate. He followed his uncle across the road and into a side street, and then by a discreet and circuitous route across the town. They went through the steep alleys and one-way streets behind the castle, up and down the worn brick pavements, skirting the Paddock where the candles were out in the horse chestnut trees, down quiet roads where branches of lilac and laburnum spilled over garden walls, until they came out out at the top of De Montfort Road.

'Where are we going, exactly?' Cooper asked, as they crossed the A275 under the high flint walls of the prison.

'It isn't far.'

They followed the bridle path that climbed slowly along the low ridge of the downs, beyond the last houses and out onto a grassy hillside. By now they had been walking for over half an hour. At last Mr Lynch struck off to the left and Cooper went after him down the hill towards a wood at the bottom of the field. At the stile in the corner Mr Lynch stopped. He looked carefully all round him and then, satisfied that there was nobody about, climbed swiftly over the stile and into the wood, motioning for Cooper to follow. It was hard going. The path was overgrown with nettles and bracken, and the ground sloped sharply away beneath their feet. Soon they left the path altogether and plunged into a thicket of young birch trees. Cooper went after his uncle, brushing aside the thin branches, and emerged at the far side to find himself standing at the top of a steep bank and looking down into a small hollow. It was overshadowed by the spreading branches of an ash tree and fringed all round with blackthorn and holly. An old green tarpaulin had been suspended from a branch of the ash tree and pegged out at the corners, making a sort of awning, beneath which a campfire was smouldering.

The bank was carpeted with wild garlic, and as Cooper scrambled down into the hollow after his uncle, trying not to snag his suit trousers on the jutting tree roots, the smell of the crushed leaves mingled with the scent of woodsmoke. They sat down on two logs that had been drawn up to the fire, either side of a battered cabin trunk. Beside Mr Lynch's seat there was a set of brass fire-irons and he unhooked the poker and stirred up the ashes. The evening sunlight slanted through the trees, making patterns on the awning overhead. All round them the birds were singing.

'You should hear them in the mornings,' Mr Lynch said. 'They're so loud you can't hear yourself think. And they're at it before the sun comes up.'

'This is where you've been living, then?'

'Of course, where did you think?'

'I thought you'd rented a furnished flat somewhere.'

'Did you really? Isn't this better?'

'Why didn't you tell me?'

'I wanted to get myself established first.' He took a kettle from a brick by the fire and stood it on a trivet over the embers. Then he opened the trunk and took out a teapot, cups and saucers, a tea strainer and a battered tin which turned out to contain biscuits. Before he pulled the lid of the trunk down and arranged the tea things on top of it, Cooper noticed various other essentials inside: a pair of wellington boots, some candles, a pile of books, a bag of potatoes and a frying pan.

'I couldn't see the point of buying a whole lot of camping things when I had a perfectly good tea set at home,' he explained. 'And anyway, I can't stand tin mugs, they burn your lips.'

'What do you do when it rains?' Cooper asked.

'That's what the awning's for. Although I haven't had a chance to try it yet – the weather's been very good so far. Just a little dew in the mornings.'

'Does anyone else know you're here?'

'No.'

'What about the landowner?'

'What about him?'

'Won't he mind?'

'I'm the landowner,' said Mr Lynch, 'and I don't mind.' And he explained how, at the auction rooms one day, he had seen a notice for a land and property sale. Among the lots one in particular had caught his eye, a two-acre plot of mixed woodland, and on the day of the auction he returned to place a bid.

'What with?' Cooper wanted to know.

'I had a little money left.'

It had cost him the last of his savings. Once again Cooper marvelled at his uncle's hidden depths: here was evidence of a remarkable resolution and boldness in action, to complement his strategic brilliance.

Mr Lynch had won the auction – in fact, he had been the only bidder. There were several parcels of woodland in the sale, and this one had attracted little interest. 'Most people are looking for something bigger,' he said. 'Five or ten acres, close to a road, with lots of mature trees. But you can't get a vehicle in here, unless you come up through the field at the bottom, and it's a bit of a stretch to call it mixed woodland. It's mostly scrub, as you can see.'

But it was precisely these qualities that attracted him. 'What I wanted was a secluded place,' he told Cooper. 'Somewhere out of the way, where I won't be disturbed. Come on, I'll show you round while the kettle's boiling.'

Mr Lynch's section of the wood was roughly triangular in shape. It extended from the edge of the field on one side down to a shallow ditch on the other, beyond which the wood continued to the bottom of the hill. On the short side of the triangle the boundary was marked by a few rotten fence posts, which were placed in a line directly down the steep slope. As they walked around he pointed out features of interest: the badgers' setts in the bottom corner, and the chalky heaps of spoil thrown up from their diggings; a promising-looking damson bush in the hedge by the stile, and the dense thickets of blackthorn and elder which screened his camp from wandering eyes.

'It was after I stopped working,' he said. 'I didn't know what to do with myself, and I didn't like being in the house on my own. I thought I'd come out here for a while, for a change of perspective, and maybe I'd work out what to do next. I spent a few nights outside, and I got to like it. I didn't plan to stay as long as this, but one thing led to another, I suppose. And I'm full of ideas – I can feel whole areas of my brain coming back to life.'

By the time they returned to the fireside the kettle was boiling, and Mr Lynch felt in one of his pockets and pulled out a few handfuls of green conifer twigs which he stuffed into the pot, before pouring boiling water over them.

'Spruce tea,' he said, handing Cooper a cup. 'It's full of vitamin C and minerals. Purifies the blood. Just the thing to drink in the evenings – it's a tonic.'

It was a pale brew with a reddish tint. Cooper took a sip. It had a sweetish, resiny taste that was not unpleasant.

'I drink it all the time now,' his uncle said. 'Have a biscuit?' He took a handful himself and passed the tin.

'How long have you been living like this?'

'A few weeks at least. Maybe a month or more. It's hard to say precisely – everything goes at a different pace in the woods, I find. Here, I'll show you. Look at your watch. What time do you make it now – the exact time?'

'Fourteen minutes past six.'

'And I make it seventeen minutes past.' He leant forward and brought his wrist next to Cooper's so they could compare the two times. 'No, don't adjust your watch. I'm always a few minutes ahead in the evenings. In the morning, I'll be a couple of minutes behind.'

Cooper was disconcerted by this. 'Are you sure you're all right?' he asked.

'What do you mean? Why shouldn't I be?'

'You just seem a little… not quite yourself.'

'Exactly right,' said Mr Lynch. 'I've never felt better.'

With this he began to tell Cooper about his new life. His days were full of event. There were always tasks to be done: fetching water, chopping wood, keeping the fire going, finding and preparing food. He had eaten mostly porridge and dried dates to begin with, but as time passed he was learning to live off the resources of the country. He washed every evening, heating water over the fire and filling an enamel washbasin. The untreated water made his skin clear and his hair thick and lustrous, like the mane of a young colt.

He slept deeply, plunging into sleep each night and waking at first light completely refreshed, without a trace of the lethargy that had dogged him every morning of his working life. For years he had suffered intermittently from mild asthma, but since moving to the woods he had felt no shortness of breath. He boasted of walking up to twenty miles in a day, and thanks to a routine of tree-climbing and wood-chopping he was stronger and fitter than he had ever been before.

'Arms like steel cables,' he said, flexing his muscles. 'Go on, feel for yourself.'

'No, thank you.'

'It's so invigorating, spending the night outdoors. It sharpens all your senses. There's a better circulation of air. In a bedroom you're removed from the world, whereas here you're in it. There's the smell of wet foliage, the flutter of wings, and when you wake in the night you can look up and see leaves and stars, not the cracks in the ceiling.'

Whether it was the tonic effect of the tea, or simply that his enthusiasm was infectious, Cooper found himself strangely moved by his uncle's account of his new life. He did look remarkably well, but it was not just that. He gave the impression of being entirely at home in his clearing, a creature in his natural habitat. There were badgers in the wood, he said, and glow-worms – he had seen them – and dormice, which made nests in the leaf-litter, and Roman snails in the clearings, on the chalk.

Much later, Cooper would remember his uncle as he appeared that evening, with the low sun slanting through the branches, glinting on the teaspoons and bathing him in a rosy glow – 'like a sage escaped from the inanity of life's battle', as Carlyle described

Coleridge in his last years on Highgate Hill. The scene was all the more touching as he seemed so ill-prepared for his new life. Even if he succeeded in escaping the attention of inquisitive ramblers and representatives of the National Parks Authority and the County Council and the National Trust, his awning and his cabin trunk would not be much help to him when the chilly mists of November blew in off the Channel and the first frosts came.

But Cooper was wrong about one thing at least. His uncle was surprisingly well equipped for life in the woods. He had studied under a man called Hornchurch, who runs a haulage company based in Crawley. Mr Hornchurch is in his forties, married with two young children, but he spends most of his weekends in an area of private woodland near Gatwick Airport, where he leads courses in survival techniques. Yes, he told me, when I rang him one morning at his office, he remembered Mr Lynch, and he would be happy to talk to me about him, but not at the office – he never had a spare moment at the office. It would be better if I came out to the woods one weekend and spoke to him there. That way I could see what it was all about.

The following Saturday afternoon I went out to the woods, where I found Mr Hornchurch with a group of his students, who were learning how to light a fire without matches, build a shelter out of fir branches and identify half a dozen common edible plants. They seemed to be enjoying themselves enormously.

They were all men. 'We do get ladies from time to time,' said Mr Hornchurch, 'but it's quite unusual, to be honest with you.'

'Why is that, do you think?'

'Women aren't so practical, I suppose.'

I did not say anything.

After the others had gone, I sat by the fire and drank a cup of raspberry-leaf tea with Mr Hornchurch. Our conversation was punctuated every few minutes by the whine of air brakes above the trees as another plane came in to land. Mr Lynch had attended several of his courses, he told me: Knife Skills, and Camp Craft, and Tracking, and Practical Botany, and Camouflage Techniques.

I asked what sort of student he had been, and Mr Hornchurch considered this before replying. He had been an outstanding pupil in many respects, he said: his shelters had been neater and drier than anyone else's, and he could get a fire going in five minutes, even in the rain. But he had made no effort to disguise his impatience with the other students. To a man, they believed themselves to be clear-sighted and grimly practical, preparing themselves for the worst, whereas he saw them as dreamers, fantasising about the imminent collapse of industrial civilisation as a means of releasing them from their dreary jobs and their mortgage repayments.

'And were they?'

'I wouldn't like to say.'

Mr Lynch's own goals were strictly practical, and once Mr Hornchurch had taught him everything he knew, he decided that the time had come to strike out on his own. He chose the site for his camp after careful deliberation, in accordance with his training. It was on well-drained ground with a southerly aspect, sheltered from the wind, with a plentiful supply of firewood and minimal risk of flood or avalanche.

Water could have been a problem. There were no streams or springs on the downs, and he did not want to drink from the water troughs or the old dew ponds which, when they are not dried up altogether, are muddied and fouled by sheep and cattle. But on one of his walks, in the middle of a field a few hundred yards out from the edge of the wood, he had come across a borehole. It had been dug originally to pump water for livestock. The pump had gone and the pipes had been disconnected, but there was still water down there. So, at first light or at dusk, he would venture out like an animal going to a waterhole, when there was just enough light to see by but least chance of being seen.

Lifting aside the metal cover he would lower a canvas bucket on a cord, weighted with a lump of flint. It took several minutes to haul it up again, hand over hand, sitting on the grass with his legs stretched out on either side of the borehole, coiling the rope as he pulled it in. He carried the bucket back to the edge of the wood and once he was safely out of sight among the trees he would decant the water into a plastic jerrycan.

The biographer D. R. Thorpe stresses the importance of place in providing an insight into character. Alec Douglas-Home, he suggests, cannot really be understood without visiting the grey towns and windswept hills of the Scottish Borders, or Sibelius without seeing the house in the countryside north of Helsinki where he lived for more than fifty years, with a sauna in the garden and a view of Lake Tuusula from his study window, or Selwyn Lloyd, who was Foreign Secretary and then Chancellor of the Exchequer under Harold Macmillan, without wandering through the streets of semi-detached Edwardian villas at West Kirby in the Wirral where he grew up. In the same way, I believe, the topography of Lewes and the surrounding countryside can help to explain the thinking and motivations of Mr Lynch.

To the casual observer the town offers a benign and tranquil prospect, with its winding streets set round a

ruined castle and surrounded by green hills. The tourist
office is fond of quoting William Morris, who once
wrote of Lewes 'lying like a box of toys under a great
amphitheatre of chalk hills'. (They omit to note that
Morris went on to describe the castle as 'not grand at
all', and the churches as 'dismally restored', concluding
'it isn't a bad country town, only not up to its position'.) But anyone who spends any time there will
see that there is more to the place than this. There is
the savage history of battles and martyrdoms. There is
the catalogue of natural disasters that have struck the
town – floods and earthquakes and once, in December
1836, an avalanche. There is the long tradition of dissent
and bloody-mindedness, best exemplified perhaps by
Thomas Paine, who worked in the town for several years
as an excise officer and kept a tobacco shop in the High
Street before leaving to foment the American and then
the French Revolution, and continued in our own time
by the bonfire societies and the anonymous exploders of
parking meters. There is a note of rawness and austerity
that can be discerned in the cries of the gulls above
Western Road, in the tidal waters of the Ouse rising
and falling in their muddy channel, and in the cold
wind off the sea that whistles through the alleyways,
up Antioch Street and Rotten Row, giving a chilly edge
even to a sunny May morning. Above all there is the

hallucinatory quality of the landscape, which lends itself to strange perspectives and dramatic effects. The steepness of the hills, humped and looming like a stage backdrop, their bareness and the lack of landmarks all play tricks with scale and distance. Seen from the High Street, the thorn bushes on Malling Down resemble a forest of mature trees, and the hillside itself appears four times higher and further away than it really is, until a few sheep wander over the brow of the hill, or a man and his dog come into view, toiling up the path, and the illusion is corrected. Or the long low building perched above the disused quarry on Cliffe Hill; from across the town, with its lights burning in a gloomy November dusk, it looks like a quarantine hospital or a research laboratory where dreadful experiments are performed, rather than what it really is – the clubhouse on Lewes Golf Course. All this I think goes some way to explaining Mr Lynch's own complexities and distorted perspectives, and suggests to me that if he had lived in any other town of a similar size in that part of the world – Sevenoaks, for example, or East Grinstead – he might not have ended up where he did.

3

A Rebel Heart

Until relatively recently, those tasked with writing the lives of public figures generally had the advantage of being able to draw on a private correspondence, whether it was a high-minded exchange of ideas over several decades like the letters between Gladstone and Henry (later Cardinal) Manning, or the torrent of intimate letters written by Herbert Asquith between 1912 and 1915 to Miss Venetia Stanley, a friend of his daughter Violet. In a non-epistolary age, this whole dimension is lacking, and the job of the biographer is more challenging as a result. If there is any extant private correspondence from this critical phase in Mr Lynch's life I have yet to discover it. But I have had the good fortune to obtain documentary evidence from an unusual source, which provides an insight into his thinking and his way of life during that time.

Returning from the woods one day he had paused

to examine a clump of red valerian growing by the side of the path when he was interrupted by a young and exceptionally silly spaniel, which ran up to him wriggling and put her paws on his knee. Her owner came up to retrieve her, and they fell into conversation. Mr Peploe was a retired telecoms engineer and the editor of the parish magazine, the *Hamsey Observer*. Impressed by the strength of Mr Lynch's interest in the natural world if not by the depth of his knowledge, he explained that he was looking for someone to write nature notes for the magazine. The local vicar, who had contributed a regular column for many years, had recently retired and left the village. Mr Lynch said that he would be happy to try, and in this way he found an occupation that gave a focus and a purpose to the long hours he spent outdoors.

His predecessor, the vicar, who used to write occasional pieces in his official capacity, had thought it prudent to adopt a pen name for the nature notes. Mr Lynch was not averse to the idea of a pen name, but he insisted on choosing it for himself, and his column appeared under the byline 'Mr Bolsover'.

'He never told me where he got it from,' Mr Peploe told me. 'I couldn't see what was wrong with "Old Brock" myself.'

But Cooper was able to shed a little light on the

choice. Bolsover Road was the name of the street in Worthing where Mr Lynch's parents-in-law used to live. When I went there I found a nondescript suburban street, two rows of semi-detached houses facing each other across a ribbon of concrete. I guessed then that 'Mr Bolsover' was one of those names chosen for being directly at odds with the thing it represents, just as Little John was the tallest of the Merry Men, or as Lev Bronshtein is said to have taken the name Trotsky from one of his jailers.

Mr Bolsover's early style, of which the following is a fair example, was modelled faithfully on that of the vicar:

At this time of year the birds are building their nests and filling the air with their song. Listen for the magpie's harsh 'chack', or the nervous laughter of the green woodpecker, which may be seen plunging its beak into the soft turf of a back garden in search of grubs and insects. The insistent piping call of the chiffchaff is unmistakable, and so is the rippling song of the skylark above open fields and downland.

But as this piece, dated 28th April, makes clear, he soon found a voice of his own:

A common sight in woods and hedgerows on the slopes of the downs are the piles of loose earth and spoil which have been excavated by badgers in the course of extending and renovating their setts. But these spoil-heaps, substantial though they are, do not really give an idea of the true scale of the networks of tunnels and chambers which extend for a considerable distance beneath the chalk. A recent report in the *Proceedings of the Sussex Field Club* describes how a badger which had been observed and tagged near Westmeston was subsequently seen emerging from a sett in Cuckoo Bottom, on the other side of the downs, having almost certainly made its way there through a tunnel that ran all the way under the escarpment – a distance of some two or three miles.

A tunnel of these dimensions would not of course have been excavated by this individual badger, but by generations of its forebears. Many of these setts have been occupied for centuries, and the most ancient diggings are thought to date from Roman times. They constitute some of the most ambitious construction projects ever undertaken in these islands, and in their scale and antiquity they are rivalled only by the great Gothic cathedrals.

Long vilified as slovenly and insanitary creatures,

badgers are in fact scrupulously clean animals, and their airy chambers present a salutary contrast to the cramped and frowsty conditions of the fox's earth. They air their bedding, bury their dead and construct communal latrines in the open air.

More remarkable even than its architectural achievements or its domestic habits are the badger's social arrangements. The colonies are small, and characterised by a high degree of equality and co-operation, without the dominance hierarchies and aggressive behaviour found among rabbits and most other social animals. It would not be too much to say that the anarchist collectives dreamed of by Kropotkin have been realised here, in the recesses of our chalk hills.

Even this relatively early offering contains features which would later be recognised as characteristic of the man. There is the unerring ability to find controversy in the most apparently innocuous of subjects, with the spirited defence of the badger's standards of hygiene. There is the magpie's erudition and, with the mention of Kropotkin at the end, the first sign of an interest in radical politics. There is also a streak of bloody-mindedness: Mr Peploe had set a limit for the nature notes of two hundred words, which this piece comfortably exceeds.

The following offering, dated 12th May, maintains the provocative tone and also offers an insight into its author's diet:

Near where I live, in a fold of the downs, there are a number of low ridges and gullies in the hillside – the remains of a Stone Age settlement. There are many such relics of the past hereabouts, and although the landscape has changed immeasurably since the time of our Mesolithic ancestors, many of the food resources that sustained them can still be found today, if we trouble to look for them. Many people will have collected blackberries on an autumn walk along the hedgerows, but who has tried the starchy and highly calorific roots of silverweed, or the seeds of fat hen, *Chenopodium album*, which can be ground and boiled into a mineral-rich gruel? We may have nibbled the leaves of wood sorrel in spring, but what of the shoots of golden saxifrage, or the sustaining tubers of the bitter vetch?

With a little effort and planning, an entire menu can be created in this way. Last week, for example, I enjoyed a banquet of pigeons' eggs baked in moss, followed by a rabbit stew flavoured with *Boletus badius* and wild marjoram and thickened with the dried pith of rosebay willowherb. This was accompanied by a stiff porridge made from the seeds of wild grasses, chiefly tufted hair-grass (*Deschampsia cespitosa*), which I had winnowed and ground to a coarse flour between two bricks, and a salad of sorrel and dandelion leaves. I finished the meal with a hatful of wild strawberries and some toasted hazelnuts, while a cup of spruce tea provided a soothing digestif.

This is perhaps not a menu for every day, but I mention it as an example of what may be achieved. Even now, armed with a sharp axe and a warm blanket, a man might live off the country indefinitely in some comfort and style.

By 5th June he was beginning to strain at the limits of the format, and addressing concerns which were more metaphysical and, with hindsight, autobiographical in nature:

In the chalk streams that rise at the base of the downs it is possible to find specimens of the larvae of several types of caddis fly. Students of natural history have always been charmed by the domestic instincts of this creature, whose first act on emerging from the egg is to assemble for itself a collection of pebbles and grit and fragments of shells and twigs and anything else it can find on the bed of the stream. It then uses these as building materials, cementing them together with an adhesive which it secretes from glands on its head to construct for itself a protective carapace.

Its industry is applauded, its craftsmanship is admired: rightly so, because the cases are beautifully constructed. But no one ever seems to mention the fact that this is only one stage in the creature's life. Having constructed its case, it withdraws. It pupates. At length it emerges as a fully developed adult, and it is at this point that the most remarkable thing of all happens. Discarding its case, leaving behind the confines of the stream bed where it has spent the whole of its life, the caddis fly takes flight, fully formed, in a glorious moment of transformation and fulfilment.

Human beings, on the other hand, are reluctant to leave the larval stage, preferring to spend their lives polishing their carapaces. But might we not find, if we had the courage to leave our homes and go out naked into the world, that we had ourselves progressed to a higher stage of development, and achieved a new level of maturity? We might create a new kind of human being in the process, one as far removed from our old selves, creeping around our houses, stirring the soup and straightening the sofa cushions, as is the adult caddis fly, dancing above the sunlit water, from the larva poking about in the waterweed and gravel.

Mr Peploe was unsure what to make of his new contributor's work at first. 'But then,' he told me, 'I started to get enquiries from people in other parishes, asking for copies of the magazine.'

Mr Peploe lives in Cooksbridge, in a bungalow across the road from the railway station. In a filing cabinet in his conservatory he keeps a copy of every issue of the *Hamsey Observer* since March 1995, when he became the editor. When I went to see him he showed me into the conservatory and took out a pile of back issues, which he spread out on the table between us. Under the table the Peploes' spaniel was sleeping in her basket.

'I realised that it might not be such a bad thing. We increased the print run, and of course that meant we got more interest from advertisers. I stopped worrying about Mr Bolsover then. I let him write whatever he wanted and I printed it. I got carried away, I suppose. I had all kinds of plans – I looked into having the magazine printed in colour. But eventually,' Mr Peploe said, 'it started to get out of hand.'

He was referring to Mr Bolsover's column for 19th June, a comparative study of the insulating properties of wool and rabbit fur. The article ran to over a thousand words, with detailed instructions on how to remove and cure the rabbit skins, but it appeared in the magazine with all but the first two paragraphs excised. 'Of course,'

Mr Peploe told me, 'I did think that people might find it too technical. But the cuts were purely a question of length. It was five times over the word limit.'

This inspired the following letter from Mr Bolsover:

Your decision to cut my latest piece reveals a degree of timidity which does the *Hamsey Observer* little credit. You say that it was too long, but I can guess the real reason. You think people will be offended by it. But what sort of fourth estate would we have in this country if editors were afraid of a few complaints? In any case, I doubt whether your readers are as delicate as you appear to believe. Their interest is not limited to the blackbird alighting on the dew-spangled turf. They want to see that blackbird tugging a worm from the dew-spangled turf and eating it, and then being swooped on by a kestrel and devoured in its turn. They want the gory details. They are agog for news of blood and violent death and copulation and the cycles of the moon. A cursory browse in the nature-writing section of any bookshop will show you that.

But whether they describe visions of the fearful Sublime as manifested in motorway embankments and sewage treatment works, or bookish rambles along the hedgerows, poking in ditches and chewing at grass stems, or epic journeys to remote tributaries of the Amazon, to banish dull care and private grief in an encounter with a jaguar and a nostrilful of hallucinogenic snuff prepared by the village headman, there is something lacking in all the accounts of the natural world that I have read. Shall I tell you what it is? They are all the work of people who are *passing through*.

There is a lot of talk these days about schemes for reintroducing wolves and bears into the wilder parts of the British Isles. I had in mind something along the same lines: to reintroduce *Homo sapiens* into the English countryside, and have him report on his experiences. What I have tried to provide for your readers is an account of the landscape written from an entirely fresh perspective – not as seen through the train window on the way to work, or walking in the woods on a Sunday afternoon, or sitting on a horse as it plods round the paddock, or fishing for carp in flooded gravel pits, or from the back of a tractor on a wet winter morning, but from the point of view of someone who inhabits it fully.

You remember the Piltdown Man, who was unearthed in a gravel pit not far from here, with the skull of a man and the jawbone of an orang-utan? A notorious hoax, of course, but don't you think there may have been a nobler motive behind his creation? Might it not express a subconscious wish to bring a new kind of person into being – one who combines, in Thoreau's words, 'the hardiness of savages with the intellectualness of the civilised man'? Why not go a little further in this vein, and give our man the sharp eyes of a kestrel, the ears of a pipistrelle bat, the olfactory receptors of a mole, the teeth of a weasel, and the digestive tract of a badger? Add to that a pair of human hands and something to write with, and you would have the ideal correspondent. Until then you will have to make do with me.

Mr Peploe did not know quite what to make of this communication, but he understood that, whatever else it might be, it was not intended as a letter of resignation. Mr Bolsover's next column arrived a week later. It was a survey of neurotoxic flora of the Weald. ('It is conjectured that the Mesolithic people of Sussex, and also Surrey and Bedfordshire, may have rendered their flint arrowheads more lethal by dipping them in a decoction prepared from the roots of *Oenanthe crocata*. I can testify that such a preparation is highly effective against small game, although I have not myself tested it on anything larger than a squirrel.')

'Don't get me wrong,' Mr Peploe said, 'I'm very open-minded about nutrition and that kind of thing. My wife went on a raw liver diet when we had our first child, and I drink rosehip tea for my circulation. But I had to draw the line somewhere. There was no question of printing it.'

'Of course not.'

'Think of the complaints. I decided to tell him at once, but when I rang it was his nephew who answered the phone, and he said that Mr Lynch had gone away. I asked how I could get in touch with him and he said he didn't have a forwarding address, but I could leave a message if I liked. I asked him if he saw Mr Lynch often, and he said hardly ever. It didn't sound very promising, but I left a message anyway, saying that I wasn't going to run his article that week. I wrote a piece of my own, about tortoiseshell butterflies, and we used that instead. Stop that!'

He was shouting at the spaniel, which had got out of its basket and was barking through the window at a cat that was stalking along the top of the garden fence.

'It can't hear you, you idiot! She's in disgrace at the moment,' Mr Peploe explained, as the dog crept back to its basket. 'Yesterday she chewed up the new tax disc for my car, and the envelope it came in. I had to go to the DVLA in Brighton to get it replaced. That took most of the morning, and last week she ate some banknotes out of my wallet – two tens and a twenty. The funny thing is, the wallet was fine. It's just the paper she goes for. Only valuable bits of paper, because we get the newspaper delivered and she's never touched that. I don't know what's got into her.

'Anyway, a few days later he came to see me. He was very angry. He wouldn't come in, so I had to talk to him across the front gate. He accused me of losing my nerve. I asked him to see it from my point of view – I said I didn't want to alienate the readers. He said it was the duty of any forward-thinking publication to try to alienate its readers, and anyway hadn't the circulation increased since he'd been writing the column? I didn't know what to say to that.' Mr Peploe gazed out of the conservatory window at the lawn. 'It was all very unpleasant, but I couldn't see that there was any alternative. All the same, I still wonder sometimes if I made the right decision.'

'What about the nature notes?'

'I write them myself now,' Mr Peploe said. 'I call myself "Reynard", but it's not the same.'

The influence of weather patterns and geological events on human affairs has been acknowledged and studied since ancient times. But the historian and the biographer alike must resist the temptation to oversimplify the mechanics of cause and effect in this regard – to claim, for example, that it was a strong El Niño effect, leading to a string of poor harvests in Europe, which sparked the French Revolution, or that the eruption of Krakatoa in 1883, which discharged vast quantities of dust into the upper atmosphere, causing particularly lurid sunsets for a number of years afterwards, was directly responsible for important breakthroughs in the work of Monet and Van Gogh.

Still, I do not think I am exceeding my brief or expressing any view that a meteorologist would find controversial when I observe that, around the time of Mr Lynch's parting of ways with Mr Peploe and the *Hamsey Observer*, an unusually strong Azores High, itself the result of unprecedented quantities of fresh water from summer ice melt in the Arctic counteracting the warming effect of the Gulf Stream, coupled with an eastward phase in the Quasi-Biennial Oscillation, resulted in a prolonged spell of wet weather across the south of England. Mr Lynch's awning must have been less effective than he had hoped, because Cooper's parents were woken on successive nights as he let himself into their house to use the tumble dryer. After nearly a week of this, they decided that they had had enough. They made no protest, but quietly had the locks changed.

A few nights later Cooper's parents were woken again, this time not by the churning of the tumble dryer but by scrabbling noises from outside. They both got out of bed, went over to the window and cautiously opened the curtains a couple of inches. Looking down, they saw Lynch trying his old key in the back door. The whole scene was brilliantly illuminated by the automatic light on the wall above the lintel. He wore a bulky overcoat and a flat cap pulled down over his eyes, obscuring his face. But then he glanced up at the window – perhaps he had sensed the curtains twitch – and for a second they saw him clearly. There was a fierce gleam in his eyes which made them recoil instinctively into the dark of the bedroom. They watched him rattling the handle in exasperation, until at last he gave up and withdrew into the shadows. All was quiet.

But when they came downstairs the next morning and looked out of the kitchen window, the view had changed. Several panels from the fence that separated their garden from the one next door were missing, and through the gap they could see part of the neighbour's lawn, her greenhouse and her vegetable patch. The fence posts were still standing, but the neighbour's winter jasmine, which had been trained all along the fence, was sprawling in the flower bed.

They went outside to inspect the damage more closely. A total of four fence panels had been taken down, and judging from the marks in the flower bed and the trail of leaves and trampled earth across the lawn they appeared to have been dragged out through the next-door garden and through the gap between the houses, where the bins were kept. The neighbour could have had nothing to do with it; she was away that week, visiting her daughter, and as Cooper's father said, even if she had been at home, she was an old woman, not in the best of health; it was hard to imagine her getting up in the middle of the night to dismantle the fence.

Then they saw that a note had been pinned to one of the fence posts. It was written on a slip of off-white laid paper that looked as though it had come from an office stationery cupboard. There was no address or company name, but *With Compliments* was printed in the bottom right-hand corner. The note read simply: *Mr Bolsover needs the fence panels.*

If the function of a *nom de guerre* is to conceal the identity of its bearer, Lynch's adoption of 'Mr Bolsover' must be counted a failure. Cooper's parents had never seen a copy of the *Hamsey Observer*, but they guessed at once who was behind the theft. They were unsettled all the same. However strange his recent behaviour might have been, Lynch had always seemed to them a man with limits. Rightly or wrongly, they felt they had the measure of him. But Mr Bolsover was a different matter. Who could say what else he was capable of, what further outrages he might be planning? And what use could he possibly have for the fence panels?

Appended to the nature notes, the name had been merely quaint. But in this new and unfamiliar context it took on an unexpectedly sinister ring. Mr Bolsover had stepped from the pages of the *Hamsey Observer*, and turned himself loose on an unsuspecting world.

4

Midnight Letters

The letters section of the *Sussex Journal* can be found towards the back of the paper, after the classified and property ads and before the local business news. Emails make up the bulk of the correspondence these days, but when Cooper first started working on the paper there was a sizeable daily postbag. He was often given the task of looking through the post before editorial meetings and winnowing out anything that appeared libellous, deranged or otherwise unsuitable for publication. It was a mundane task, but Cooper found it soothing to sit at his desk in a corner of the office with a paper-knife in his hand, slicing open the envelopes and sorting the letters into piles.

He was occupied in this way one morning, opening the post and half listening to what was going on around him. From all sides came the noise of fingers scuttling over keyboards. Through the partition wall he could hear Mr Critchley, the editor, sighing as he examined the accounts. Bancroft, the news editor, who had a permanent cold, was snuffling and blowing his nose at the desk opposite. Tilling, the senior reporter, was eating a sausage roll, distributing crumbs evenly across his desk, his computer keyboard and his shirt front, and telling an interminable story about finding a doll's house at a car boot sale. Cooper had already opened three letters which set out conflicting but strongly held opinions about proposals for an all-weather sports pitch in East Grinstead, and one pleading for information that might lead to the arrest of a Newhaven man who had been seen chasing ducks with a butterfly net. Then he opened the next envelope and found this:

Sir, In view of the upward trend in the price of basic groceries such as flour, meat and vegetables, I would like to share with your readers the results of an interesting culinary experiment.

For several months now I have been cooking and eating rats on a regular basis, and I can testify that their flesh is sweet, lean and easily digestible. They can be prepared in a variety of ways, and a brace of large rats will feed a family of four. After trying my Flash-fried Rat with Watercress Salad and my Rat Confit in a Mushroom and Red Wine Gravy, my friends assure me that they now prefer a fine fat rat to a chicken.

Rats are easily trapped (I favour a baited cage in a storm drain) and they are freely available. If every local household dined on rat once a week they would have not only a healthy supplement to their diet but also the satisfaction of knowing that they were helping to reduce the rodent population of our town, something that the council's Pest Control Unit has conspicuously failed to do.

Mr Bolsover, Lewes

When this letter was passed round at the editorial meeting it caused a stir among Cooper's colleagues. They were used to receiving eccentric letters – it was an occupational hazard. But this bore none of the familiar hallmarks. It was not written in green or purple ink. There were no sequins in the envelope. It was neither ranting nor incoherent. It was provocative, but it contained a kernel of sense. It was written in black ballpoint, on plain white writing paper.

'A good steady hand,' said Mr Bancroft, who took an interest in these things. 'Might be an engineer, or a bank manager. And I'll bet you anything you like he's an Aquarius. I can tell by the size of the loops.'

When it appeared in the newspaper, the letter provoked a flood of correspondence in reply. A doctor from Kingston wrote that rats were a health hazard, even if thoroughly cooked. A Mr J. C. of Seaford disputed the claim that rats were easily trapped, writing that in his experience the best way to catch rats was with a well-trained terrier, while the director of the Pest Control Unit angrily defended his team's record in dealing with rodent infestations.

A few days later, a second letter arrived:

Sir, May I congratulate the Borough Council on its recently announced policy of installing seatbelts on all school buses (article 9th April)? This safety measure will be welcomed by all right-thinking parents, but in my view it does not go far enough.

I would like to see the scheme extended by fitting seatbelts in all school classrooms, as an aid not to road safety but to discipline. The seatbelts would be remote-locking and centrally controlled by the teacher. We have the technology – why not use it? This simple expedient would not only improve classroom behaviour but also slash truancy rates, as persistent absentees could be confined at their desks overnight.

And the following week:

Sir, An article in last week's paper blames the shortage of affordable housing in Lewes on a lack of suitable land for new developments and on planning controls which, already rigorous, have only become more restrictive since the town's incorporation in the South Downs National Park. As the article suggests, any solution must achieve the apparently impossible feat of combining a high density of housing units with minimal impact on the landscape.

I do not pretend to have any practical experience in the field of architecture, construction or town planning, but given that the experts have failed so far to address the problem I am emboldened to offer a suggestion of my own.

I propose to excavate a number of cave dwellings in the disused chalk quarry on the Cliffe industrial estate on the west side of the town. The cliff here is approximately two hundred feet high, and I estimate that it would be possible to incorporate forty or fifty units in this space, spread over several levels. The old quarries at Offham and on the north side of Malling Hill offer the potential for expansion with similar developments.

The practical advantages of the scheme are numerous. The houses would be cheap to build, secure and easily insulated. The views, from the higher caves especially, would be spectacular. The quarry is a brownfield site, and as far as impact on the landscape is concerned, I believe the scheme would realise the vision set out by Edward Carpenter in *Civilisation: Its Cause and Cure* of 'dwelling places so simple and elemental in character that they will fit in the nooks of the hills or along the banks of the streams or by the edges of the woods without disturbing the harmony of the landscape or the songs of the birds'.

There would also be a wider aesthetic benefit. I do not want to overstate the case, but it seems to me that a development of this kind would revolutionise the practice of architecture in this country. The classical style is dead – a ragbag of exhausted motifs. As for modernism, the last hundred years have been a cul-de-sac. But here we have a fresh method. This is architecture as excavation, not construction. A new vernacular which is innovative, yet rooted in tradition, and whose points of reference are the anthill, the badger's sett, the root cellar and the ice house. In short, an entirely new strand in our national architecture.

I have prepared a detailed proposal with initial costings, which I would be happy to present to the Borough Council or to any private company or individual who might be interested in implementing the scheme.

That week it took Cooper three times longer than usual to go through the postbag, the letters page was almost entirely given over to correspondence relating to Mr Bolsover, and there was a noticeable increase in the paper's circulation and in traffic to its website. Mr Critchley was delighted.

Perhaps Mr Bolsover was encouraged as well because more letters from him followed, with increasing frequency: first at a rate of two or three a week, then daily, until at one point several were arriving each day. Gladstone's mind is described by Philip Magnus, one of his many biographers, as one in which 'the tensions of the age seethed in molten fury', and anyone reading this correspondence will discern a similar tumult in the mind of Mr Bolsover. None of the letters was stamped or postmarked. They came in plain envelopes, with 'By Hand' written in the corner, and they were stuffed through the letterbox at night, to be found on the mat by the first person in to the office, along with the pizza delivery leaflets and the cards from taxi firms. I quote below the openings of a few, to give an idea of the range of their author's concerns:

Sir, Cobbett writes in his *Cottage Economy* that 'a nation is made powerful and to be honoured in the world, not so much by the number of its people as by the ability and character of that people'. Can we not conclude from this that given a sufficient degree of ability and character, an individual might constitute a nation mightier and more worthy of honour than the great powers of the world?…

Sir, Has it occurred to you that *Don Quixote* is the most significant work of political theory ever written? It is more profound than Plato's *Republic*, more pragmatic than Machiavelli, more comprehensive than the works of Karl Marx …

Sir, Your readers would do well to heed the warning of John Stuart Mill: 'That so few now dare to be eccentric marks the chief danger of our time …'

Sir, I have taken up arms against a sea of troubles …

Much of what Mr Bolsover wrote was, as Mr Critchley put it, 'a red rag to pedants and moralisers', but the appeal of his correspondence was broader and deeper than that. The letters conveyed the impression of a man with great seriousness of purpose, even though it was far from obvious what that purpose might be. It was impossible to trace a clear line of argument or discover a settled position in the correspondence, and each new letter only made the picture more complex and intriguing: the author was not a revolutionary, or a joker, or a philosopher, or a madman, but a combination of all these characters at once.

In the newspaper offices there was considerable speculation about the identity and motives of Mr Bolsover. Cooper kept his own counsel about this, but his colleagues' fascination had given him an idea. For some time he had been chafing at the restrictions imposed on a junior reporter. In a fortnight he had only been out of the office once, to cover a football match in Division Five of the Kent and Sussex Youth League (Under-11s) between the East Hoathly Predators and the Crowhurst Wildcats (it was a feature of the league that team names were chosen by a popular vote among the players). Bancroft lived in East Hoathly, and in this particular match his son was playing at left back for the Predators. It gave Cooper a certain satisfaction to report that he had been substituted early in the second half, and that the Wildcats won by three goals to one.

But it was not enough. Cooper craved a bigger story, and now he had found one. As the only person who knew the true identity of Mr Bolsover, he was in an ideal position to conduct an exclusive interview.

His uncle agreed to the idea at once. He was glad of the opportunity to speak his mind, and he did so at length. As Cooper was not entirely confident in his note-taking abilities, he asked if he could make a video recording of their conversation by way of insurance. Mr Bolsover agreed, on condition that he could choose the location himself, and the interview took place in a clearing in the woods near Offham, some distance from his actual camp. It was early evening, and the rooks were coming in to roost, cawing in the trees above their heads. Later that night when Cooper started to transcribe the conversation, he could hear them in the background as he played through the recording.

Cooper had been worried that if he consulted Mr Critchley about the interview beforehand, the editor might reject his idea or, which would be worse, that he would assign the story to another reporter. He decided that it would be safer not to say anything until he had done the interview and written it up.

'Frankly,' said Mr Critchley, when Cooper presented him with the finished article, 'I've been wondering if it isn't time to stop printing letters from this man. Of course, it's been very good for the paper, all this debate. But people will get tired of it. The letters page is meant to be the mouthpiece of the readers. We can't have it turned into one man's personal soapbox. And you want me to run an interview of – what is this? A thousand words? Don't you think he's had enough encouragement?'

'We can trim it.'

'I'm sorry,' Mr Critchley said. 'If you'd come to me with this two weeks ago, I'd have said it was a good idea. But it's not enough to have a good idea – you need it at the right time. Timing is everything in journalism. The sooner you learn that the better.'

Cooper had recorded the interview on his phone, and not wanting his efforts to have been entirely wasted, he posted the transcript and a short clip from the video on his blog. This was a new venture which he had started on the advice of Tilling, the senior reporter, with the aim of raising his professional profile. But he lacked his colleague's talent for self-promotion, and so far he had only posted an account of his post-match conversation with the coach of the East Hoathly Predators and a short piece about a village fête.

In the same week that Cooper had his discussion with Mr Critchley, a conference was held at the University of Sussex ('New Directions in Social Theory') at which the philosopher Jean-Joseph Berceau had been invited to speak. Professor Berceau was a former lecturer in epistemology and moral philosophy at the École Normale Supérieure in Paris and visiting professor at Stanford University, but despite his formidable credentials he had always seen himself as a champion of voices from outside the academy. During the plenary discussion that followed his conference address, he was asked by a member of the audience for his views on Mr Bolsover. Professor Berceau was not a habitual reader of the *Sussex Journal*, and had never heard of Mr Bolsover, but he was intrigued, and that night he looked up Mr Bolsover's correspondence on the newspaper's website. He had a couple of days to spare after the conference finished, which he had been planning to spend visiting friends in London, but he decided to change his plans. He sent a message via the paper, asking for a meeting. In Mr Bolsover's rejection of conventional values, the professor wrote, in his provocations, in his impatience with folly and pretence, he resembled the great Greek philosopher Diogenes.

Mr Bolsover grumbled at this comparison, saying that it was a little too fulsome for his taste, and that at all events he was better dressed than Diogenes, who had been in the habit of going about naked. But it seemed to Cooper that he was pleased all the same by the prospect of a symposium. He instructed Cooper to set out a couple of deckchairs in the back garden at Barcombe Crescent and sent him to fetch the professor from the station.

Professor Berceau was something of an Anglophile. He had spent the academic year of 1970–71 as a French-language assistant at a grammar school in Folkestone, where he had acquired his virtually flawless English and gained a black belt in karate. He was also a contrarian of long standing. During the events of May 1968, when his fellow students at the University of Paris-Nanterre had occupied the lecture halls and administration buildings and shut down the campus, he staged a sit-in of his own to protest against the sit-in. Soon after that, he had narrowly avoided being forced by an angry crowd to eat the toggles from his own duffel coat after being seized by an uncontrollable urge to chant 'Down with Ho Chi Minh' at an anti-Vietnam War demonstration.

All the same, he and Bolsover eyed each other warily as they shook hands. They made a striking pair, Cooper thought: the one dressed in an old overcoat with a worn velvet collar, corduroy trousers and thick socks stuffed into galoshes, the other in an artfully crumpled suit and a white shirt with the top three buttons undone. Each suspected the other of having dressed up for the occasion; each was wrong.

They went into the garden, where Cooper brought them tea. He took no part in the conversation, but watched them through the kitchen window. He could not tell how the meeting was going, although he noticed that they sat for long periods without saying anything at all. Later they got up and walked round the garden, pausing at the fence, where Bolsover cut a sprig of jasmine and put it in the professor's buttonhole. They also stopped to examine Cooper's vegetable patch – the professor made some remark and Bolsover laughed. At last they asked Cooper to ring for a taxi, and while they waited for it to arrive they took turns shooting darts from Bolsover's blowpipe at a net of peanuts Cooper had suspended from the bird table.

After Berceau had gone, Mr Bolsover offered nothing to Cooper about their conversation, but the professor gave his own account in an article which he wrote shortly afterwards. I quote a few extracts below:

First impressions: some strength in the handshake. Rubber overshoes. A straw hat with a broken crown. The costume of an English eccentric. But this is a man who has gone the distance…

We meet in a suburban garden with laurel hedge and deckchairs. Incongruous environment for a latter-day Thoreau. But we are the guests of an admirer of his – a tongue-tied youth of about twenty, who brings us tea. And then retreats, to what he perhaps considers a safe distance. For the rest of the afternoon he watches us from the kitchen window…

His antecedents: without doubt he owes something to Thoreau, but I also detect the influence of the English radical tradition. He speaks with admiration of William Blake and Edward Carpenter, two visionaries for whom social reform began with a willingness to experiment in their own lives. His own approach is equally uncompromising, and I do not hesitate to call him a radical, but one of a particularly contemporary stamp – a *post-ideological* radical...

I ask whether the ideas of Foucault and Guy Debord have played a large part in his calculations. A blank look. He affects not to understand what I'm talking about. With an air of perfect gravity he goes back to describing a project for making people live in caves which has received, so he claims, serious consideration from the authorities. And I think, yes, I am in the presence of genius. Or rather: we are both in the presence of genius, but only one of us knows it.

The cultural critic P. D. Kahn, writing in the *New York Times*, gave this article a spirited rebuttal. Describing Berceau's analysis as 'a display of breathtaking superficiality', he observed that if Mr Bolsover had any politics at all it was clearly a half-baked rural anarchism in the mould of the seventeenth-century Diggers, with no more relevance to contemporary global politics than the divine right of kings. It was only his misfortune, Kahn concluded, to have been chosen as the subject for one of Professor Berceau's masterclasses in intellectual posturing.

This high-minded international exchange brought Mr Bolsover and his activities to the attention of a wider audience, which soon found its way to Cooper's blog, and his video was seen by a steadily increasing number of viewers. The video shows Mr Bolsover sitting with his back against the trunk of an oak tree, holding a willow-pattern cup and saucer, and talking for a few minutes animatedly to camera. At the end of the interview he reaches up to grasp a low branch and pulls himself into the tree. The camera follows him until he is lost in the canopy.

All these elements were intriguing: the incongruity of the willow-pattern china in the woodland setting, the intensity of Mr Bolsover's expression, and above all the extraordinary speed and agility with which he climbed the tree at the end. But the video attracted the attention of the press for other reasons. They sensed a story behind it. Who was this man? What was he doing in the woods, and what would become of him?

The journalists came first in ones and twos with note-books, with sound recorders and microphone booms. They made discreet enquiries in the town and then set out to explore the surrounding fields and woods, until it seemed that there was a bedraggled reporter poking in every ditch, staking out every copse and lurking behind every hedge. They were followed by camera crews and mobile broadcasting units, who were soon lured by their sat-nav equipment down impassable lanes and muddy farm tracks, or became so demoralised by the complexities of the town's one-way system that they parked in any available spaces in the quiet residential streets behind the castle, where traffic wardens waited gleefully to give them tickets.

They did not find Mr Bolsover, but in his absence they went in search of the glade and the oak tree where his interview had been recorded. They analysed his letters and found him to be, variously, an extrovert with obsessive-compulsive tendencies and a mildly neurotic introvert. They tracked down Mr Hornchurch and interviewed him at his office in Crawley. After he had obliged them by demonstrating some basic fire-lighting techniques for the camera, striking sparks from a firesteel onto a handful of tinder which he took out of his desk drawer, they asked about Bolsover's chances of survival. Mr Hornchurch leant back in his swivel chair and looked thoughtful. Mr Bolsover had been one of his best students, he said, but the English countryside could be a perilous environment for the unwary. There was the danger of inadvertently eating one of the many inoffensive-looking but lethal species of fungi and berries, the possibility of contracting any number of waterborne diseases, and the more prosaic but equally deadly threat of hypothermia when the weather turned colder. There was also the risk, even here, of attack by wild animals; he knew a man, camping out in the New Forest, whose toes had been partially eaten by a fox while he slept. Anyone who coped with these immediate hazards was likely to succumb in the longer term to the complications of various mineral and vitamin deficiencies.

As the source of the video, Cooper was a natural point of contact for the press, and he found himself fielding requests for information about Mr Bolsover's background and whereabouts, which he ignored, and overtures of various kinds, which he passed on to his uncle. These included an invitation to write nature notes for *Vogue*, several enquiries about the film rights to his life story, questionnaires from lifestyle magazines asking him to name the five items in his wardrobe that he could not live without, an offer of a contract to write his autobiography and a request to endorse a range of vicious-looking survival knives.

Cooper had approached Mr Critchley with an idea for another article on how Mr Bolsover was reacting to the extraordinary levels of public interest in him, only to be told that the story was now too important to be entrusted to a junior reporter. He was not disappointed, therefore, when his uncle rejected all the overtures made to him. But he was as surprised as anyone else by Mr Bolsover's final letter to the *Sussex Journal*:

Sir, I intend no slur on your publication when I say that I have come to the conclusion that the pages of a newspaper are no longer a suitable forum in which to advance my ideas, and I have decided to go into politics.

This announcement was received with great interest by representatives of the main political parties, each of whom had good reason, as they saw it, to consider him one of their own. The Conservative Association had been impressed by the bracingly disciplinarian tone of some of his letters to the newspaper. The members of the Labour group on the County Council could point to his piece on the communal life of badgers as evidence of progressive tendencies, and they had written to the party's National Executive Committee suggesting that Mr Bolsover should be put up as a Labour candidate in the next general election against one of the many cabinet ministers who would be defending marginal seats. His mention of John Stuart Mill, meanwhile, had convinced the local Liberal Democrats that he was essentially a political liberal. The Liberal Democrat MP for Lewes had recently announced his intention to retire at the next election, and they believed that if Mr Bolsover could be persuaded to stand in his place they would have a good chance of holding the seat.

At this critical juncture Mr Bolsover issued a statement which dashed all their hopes. He thanked everyone who had taken an interest in his political ambitions. But the general election, he said, was more than two years away, and he was not prepared to wait that long. He was eager to plunge into the fray at once: there was no time to be lost. He had therefore decided to contest the forthcoming by-election on Lewes Borough Council, which had been called following the retirement of Dr Savidge, a popular and long-serving councillor in the Winterbourne ward, on the grounds of ill health. The main parties had already chosen their candidates for this by-election, and in any case he did not feel that any of their programmes was quite in keeping with his own political outlook. In view of this, he had decided to stand as an independent.

5

The Hinge of Fate

The Borough of Lewes comprises the town of Lewes itself, the surrounding countryside within a radius of about five miles, the valley of the River Ouse, the coastal towns of Peacehaven, Newhaven and Seaford, and the villages of Chailey, Plumpton, Wivelsfield and Ditchling to the north and east. Winterbourne ward is similarly divided between town and country, incorporating the southern suburbs of Lewes and an area of marsh and downland immediately outside the town bisected by the A27. The census taken in 2011 recorded 2,194 households, of which just over sixty per cent were owner-occupied. At the last election there had been 3,237 registered voters.

Mr Bolsover's campaign began on the morning after he announced his candidature. Unlike his opponents, who had jobs to go to and could only campaign in the evenings, he was free to spend the whole of his day knocking on people's doors, and this was exactly what he did. For a man of his gregarious nature the idea of walking the streets and trying to engage strangers in conversation was appealing, especially after his long spell of relative isolation in the woods, and he proved to be a tireless and dedicated campaigner.

On the whole he was well received. His letter-writing had aroused people's curiosity, and being an independent candidate undoubtedly helped him, because he did not have to bear the burden of his party's past failures and broken promises, so there were no reproaches about not catching criminals, improving the roads or emptying the bins. Besides, no one assumed they knew what he stood for, which made them more disposed to listen to him. The independent candidate is always an unknown quantity, and this worked to Mr Bolsover's advantage.

He also possessed a smile of considerable charm and a firm dry handshake, both of which he deployed to good effect, and which perhaps compensated for his distinctly combative conversational manner. As he explained to Cooper, he did not want to insult the voters' intelligence by attempting to ingratiate himself purely in order to solicit their support. It was precisely his readiness to espouse unpopular views, to argue with the electors, to alienate and insult them even, which demonstrated his unwavering commitment to democratic principles.

His rhetoric went down well at many addresses. Disciplinarians liked it when he spoke of 'clearing the vermin off the streets'; they had no idea that he meant it literally, with his plan for trapping rats in the storm drains. Old ladies told him that his hands were warm. Romantics were impressed by this grizzled woodsman in his battered work boots and his old grey jacket whose capacious and bulging pockets hinted at the presence of concealed weapons or illegally taken game.

In fact, the bulges were bundles of campaign leaflets. He handed these out in a mechanical way, more as a token of his legitimacy than anything else, like a policeman flashing his badge. They provided little information about his policies, and as such they were ideal for his purposes, as they left him free to extemporise when he was out canvassing on whatever topic happened to be on his mind, with no danger that he might contradict what was written in the campaign literature.

It is instructive to compare Mr Bolsover's leaflets with the glossy flyers, all photographs and bullet points, that were being circulated by his opponents. Kate Rowlandson, the Labour candidate, was pictured crouching in the road and pointing at a pothole. The Liberal Democrat, Steven Gillray, was shown meeting local residents, while the Conservative candidate appeared in one photograph shaking hands with the Mayor of London and in another standing in shirtsleeves at the open door of a garden shed, above the mystifying caption 'Neil Cruikshank is determined to protect the unique character of our area.' I felt, studying the leaflets, that going by the pledges and the policies alone, without the photo-graphs and the party templates, it would have been difficult to tell the other candidates apart. 'Responding to Residents' was Mr Gillray's slogan. Mr Cruikshank had gone for 'Action, Not Words', and 'Your Priorities are My Priorities', while the Labour leaflet had 'Fighting For Your Community'. All expressed concern about the state of the roads. Mr Cruikshank believed that the speed bumps in Railway Lane were a safety hazard, and wanted them 'restored to their former style and size'. Dr Rowlandson wanted more gritting lorries, and so did Mr Gillray, while all three called for urgent action on potholes. As for the traffic-calming measures on Railway Lane, Mr Gillray kept an open mind: 'Bollards may be the answer.'

Mr Bolsover made no promises. In his campaign literature there were no accounts of his good works, and no cataloguing of his opponents' incompetence and venality. A slogan on one flyer, 'Improvement makes straight roads, but the crooked roads without Improvement are roads of Genius', was taken by some as a statement of policy on highway maintenance, but it was actually a quotation from William Blake's *Marriage of Heaven and Hell*. Other flyers bore quotations from the Book of Proverbs: 'Where there is no vision, the people perish,' and from Thoreau's *Civil Disobedience*: 'That government is best which governs not at all.' They were written in block capitals on sheets of lined paper torn from an exercise book, and once in felt tip on a large maple leaf.

It was Cooper's job to print the leaflets. He had misgivings about the design and even more about the printing method, which involved running off as many copies as he thought he could get away with after hours on the overworked photocopier in the newspaper office. But the fact is that the leaflets were exactly in keeping with the style of Mr Bolsover's campaign. It did not matter that they were rendered illegible in places by the murky pall that the photocopier imparted. Eccentric, intriguing, a little rough around the edges, they fitted perfectly with his demeanour on the doorstep.

In the week before the election Cooper helped out by riding round on his bicycle in the evenings to deliver campaign leaflets. One night when he went to fetch it from the shed he found that there was something wrong with the pedals. He took it into the garden to examine it more closely and discovered that the bottom bracket had been dismantled, and the ball bearings removed.

'Probably thieves,' Mr Bolsover said when Cooper told him about it. 'They're always going into garden sheds. Have you put a lock on that shed? No? Well, it would be easy enough to get in.'

'Wouldn't they have taken the whole bike? And why didn't they take anything else? The lawnmower, for instance.'

'That's just my guess,' he said. 'I really couldn't say. Have you reported it?'

'No.' It was an old bike, and Cooper did not use it very often. It was several weeks before he got round to having it fixed.

'Just as well.'

The climax of the election campaign came a few days before polling day, when a meeting was held in St Mary's Church Hall for all the candidates to meet the voters and answer their questions. The church hall was furnished with a battered linoleum floor, children's paintings on the walls and stacks of plastic chairs. The evening began with refreshments in the form of ginger biscuits and cups of tea, and an opportunity for the voters to circulate and to chat informally with the candidates. This was to be followed by a panel discussion, convened by Mrs Margaret Finch, MBE, the chair of the Winterbourne Community Group.

The Labour candidate sat at a round table covered with leaflets. She was campaigning for a network of cycle paths and a twenty-mile-per-hour speed limit outside schools, but she spoke without conviction. In the previous two elections her party had come third, and she must have known that her chances of winning were slender. Even her latest leaflet struck a defeatist note: 'Every vote for Kate Rowlandson will send a message that these campaigns mustn't be ignored.' Mr Cruikshank, in the Conservative corner, was a bright-eyed, balding man in his thirties. He had come straight from work ('Neil is a partner in an investment firm'), and had not changed out of his suit. The Liberal Democrat, Mr Gillray, had wayward grey hair and a dreamy expression, but having served two terms on the Borough Council in the 1990s he had the benefit of experience. He sat slumped in his chair as if wishing himself elsewhere, while a couple harangued him on the subject of bollards.

Although the meeting was well attended, only a minority of the people there were registered voters. The rest were curious residents of neighbouring wards and members of the press. It was Mr Bolsover they had come to see, and the other candidates were largely ignored as everyone clustered round him.

Until this point the attitude of his opponents towards Mr Bolsover had been ambivalent. They resented his rejection of their parties' overtures, but at the same time each of them was relieved that he had not chosen to throw in his lot with one of their opponents. They despised him as an outsider with no real understanding of local politics and were frankly envious of the publicity he had managed to attract, but they hoped to make use of it to communicate their own messages. The contest was close enough that if Mr Bolsover garnered even a small number of votes it might make a difference to the outcome, and they were determined to ensure that any votes he did obtain would be at the expense of their rivals. Their strategy would be to focus their energies on attacking the other parties and to ignore him altogether.

But they were dismayed by the stark proof that evening of the public's continued interest in Mr Bolsover, and when the panel discussion began they turned on him in a pack. Mr Gillray, who was the favourite to win the election, showed himself to be far less abstracted than he had appeared in the first part of the evening, and was particularly energetic in his attacks. With the wisdom born of experience, he had been saving himself for the panel discussion. Mr Bolsover had arrived wearing a beret and a fortnight's growth of beard. He had removed the beret when he came in, but it was probably his appearance which caused Mr Gillray, during a heated exchange about bicycle paths, to refer to him acidly as 'the Che Guevara of the Home Counties'.

Mr Bolsover retorted that he was nothing like Che Guevara, who had been, in his words, 'a natural conservative', and that Sussex was not one of the Home Counties, as he would know if he had ever studied the Green Belt (London and Home Counties) Act 1938.

Perhaps, then, Mr Cruikshank suggested, he would like to tell everyone which political figures he did admire.

Without hesitation Mr Bolsover named Lord Salisbury, Queen Victoria's last prime minister.

Amid the general murmur of surprise and disbelief, he went on to explain. It was not the details of Salisbury's policies that Mr Bolsover admired, but his guiding principles. Salisbury had a deep aversion to officials and lawmakers. He took a quietist approach to government, and was contemptuous of those who believed that a government's effectiveness is directly proportional to the number of laws it passes.

There was also his appearance. Salisbury's luxuriant, flowing beard and the great balding dome of his head lent him an air of immense gravitas, as did his pensive expression: his portraits generally showed him lost in thought, as though pondering important matters of state. This was in direct contrast to his great contemporary and rival Gladstone who posed for photographs looking, so Mr Bolsover said, warming to his theme, 'like an indignant owl', and whose bristling side-whiskers appeared merely eccentric to modern eyes. Both men, however, presented a salutary contrast to the moon-faced children who held political office today. And Salisbury had been a supreme pragmatist: not for him the lethal devotion to an ideology at the expense of everything else. 'The axioms of the last age are the fallacies of the present,' he once wrote. 'There is nothing abiding in political science but the necessity for truth, purity and justice.'

After Mr Bolsover finished speaking there was silence. Mr Gillray asked whether the constituents could expect a similarly laissez-faire approach if he won the election, and Mrs Finch tried to get the discussion going again by asking the panel for their views on how to enforce the regulation that dogs should be kept on leads in the Paddock. But Mr Bolsover's monologue had left everyone curiously chastened, and the meeting broke up soon afterwards.

From Mr Bolsover's interest in political giants of the Victorian era, the reader may get the impression that he was a man out of his time. I think that he was, but I don't believe he was especially nostalgic for the nineteenth century, and I find it hard to identify a time and place where he would have felt at home. Eighteenth-

17 Barcombe Crescent

An early bivouac

The outdoor swimming pool

*The oak tree in which many of Mr Bolsover's
letters were written*

A view of Mr Bolsover's constituency

The constituency proposed by Cooper – the rotten borough

The site of Mr Bolsover's camp, as it appears today

A view from Mr Bolsover's dugout

century North America might have suited him, during the chaos of the Seven Years War, roaming the boundless woods that stretched along the Hudson River, beyond the reach of any law. I can imagine him too in Russia in 1917, leading a minor faction in St Petersburg before the Bolsheviks took over the revolution, when it was still possible to believe in the imminent creation of a new heaven and a new earth.

But even in these apparently congenial places I doubt whether he would really have fitted in. Among the wolves and bears and woodsmen of the American frontier he would have pined for more stimulating company, and I suspect that his faction in the Russian Revolution would have been a faction of one. Perhaps the truth is that he was nostalgic not for the past but for some future time – and that is, after all, one definition of a visionary.

In the last days before the election the campaign took on a new intensity, and all the candidates were out canvassing every evening. Despite himself, Cooper began to be caught up in the drama of it. His uncle had been driving himself hard for weeks and he was beginning to show signs of fatigue. He kept himself going on spruce tea and dried dates, but his voice was hoarse from all the speeches he had made, he complained of cramp in his fingers from shaking so many people's hands, and his feet were sore from walking. 'It's not the distance,' he told Cooper, 'I'm used to the distance, it's walking on pavements that does it. I hardly ever walk on solid surfaces these days.' Early on the morning of the election he and Cooper went round the polling stations together. A few people were out voting already, but the exit polls at that early stage were inconclusive. Unable to stand the tension any longer, Bolsover set out by himself for a long walk, while Cooper went off to work.

They met again that night at the count, which took place in the sports hall of the local secondary school. It was a large space, with capacity for several hundred students at morning assembly, but it was full. The usual audience of party officials and spouses and election agents was supplemented by a large contingent of journalists. None of them seriously expected an upset but they felt that whatever the result, the evening represented a climax to Mr Bolsover's whole project, and even those news organisations which had not paid much attention to his progress so far were determined not to miss it. Cooper's colleague Mr Tilling was there for the *Sussex Journal*, along with the political correspondents of several national newspapers and a television news team.

Cooper arrived just as the count was finishing. He had hoped for a word with his uncle before the results were announced, but by the time he had pushed his way through the crowd the returning officer was already standing on the stage at the far end of the hall and signalling for the candidates to join her. They clambered onto the stage and formed a row of tired faces and party rosettes, with Mr Bolsover at the end. He was wearing jeans tucked into work boots, a leather jerkin and a straw hat that was unravelling at the brim. He leant forward, glanced along the line of candidates, caught Cooper's eye and winked.

The returning officer began to read out the results. Steven Gillray, the Liberal Democrat candidate, had received 217 votes. Kate Rowlandson, the Labour candidate, had received 96 votes. Neil Cruikshank, the Conservative candidate, had received 163 votes. And Mr Bolsover had received 482 votes.

The sense of shock and incredulity in the sports hall was palpable. Mr Gillray, who despite the challenge from Mr Bolsover had been expecting to win comfortably, looked as if he might faint. Mr Cruikshank, who had taken exception during the campaign to what he saw as Bolsover's appropriation of Lord Salisbury, was furious. Even Dr Rowlandson's face had fallen. She had not expected to win, but she had hoped that with an unknown independent standing against her she would not come last.

But what impressed Cooper most was the expression on his uncle's face as the result was announced. He was the only person in the room who did not look surprised. Only then did Cooper understand that he had been expecting to win all along. Mr Bolsover took off his hat, shook hands with each of the defeated candidates and then the returning officer, and stepped forward to the microphone.

In the course of his subsequent career as a journalist, Cooper told me, he had attended more late night election counts than he cared to remember, at school halls and council offices across the south of England, and listened to countless speeches by newly elected councillors rendered all but incoherent by elation and lack of sleep. But he never again heard a speech like the one Mr Bolsover gave that night.

He began conventionally enough, by thanking the returning officer and her staff for their efficiency, the police for manning the polling stations, and the other candidates for fighting their campaigns on the issues. But instead of leaving it at that or going on, as the more effusive speakers sometimes did, to restate his key policy goals or pledge to work tirelessly for all residents of the ward, whether or not they had voted for him, Mr Bolsover launched into a ferocious attack on his constituents.

'There are more than three thousand people on the electoral roll in this ward,' he told his audience, 'and barely a thousand of them have bothered to cast their votes. This equates to a turnout of less than thirty per cent. Even by the standards of local elections, this figure is disgracefully low. In truth, this result is a victory not for me but for apathy and disengagement. Voting figures like this make a mockery of representative democracy. If the people of Winterbourne ward woke tomorrow morning to find that their affairs were being run by some crazed demagogue unfit to hold public office, it would be no more than they deserve.'

He made no mention of his political views or his plans for government, and indeed it would have been unnecessary for him to do so. The attack on the voters who had just elected him was a perfect demonstration of his ruling principle. Emerson's comment on Thoreau, that he was never truly himself 'except in opposition', could equally well have been applied to Mr Bolsover.

The journalists had their headlines now: WINNING CANDIDATE SLAMS VOTERS FOR 'DISGRACEFUL' TURNOUT and COUNCIL SEAT FOR 'CRAZED DEMAGOGUE'? When Mr Bolsover finished speaking they pressed forward, desperate for a word with him. But he had his exit prepared. He picked up a chair and made for the door at the side of the stage, and by the time they had scrambled up the steps and across the cluttered stage after him he was through the door and halfway down the hallway on the other side, closing the door to the boys' toilets and wedging it shut with the chair. They hammered at the door but there was no response, and by the time they had managed to force it open they saw that they were too late. The metal-framed window at the far end, comfortably big enough for a man to climb through, was open to the night, and Mr Bolsover had gone.

6

Platitudes and Rosewater

Like all newly elected councillors, Mr Bolsover was entitled to office space in the council building. This was an undistinguished mock-Georgian structure on the edge of town with a view of the railway line and the station car park. Each of the three main parties had an office of its own, shared by all its councillors, which became more or less cramped as the number of seats it held on the council rose and fell. There was no designated office for independent councillors, as it was several years since one had been elected, but after some deliberation a small storeroom next to the kitchen on the second floor was identified as being suitable. It was cleared out to make room for Mr Bolsover.

Cooper visited him there one day and found it snug but cupboard-like. There was just enough room for a desk, a chair and a filing cabinet. On the wall above the desk hung two black-and-white photographs of men with beards. One was Lord Salisbury and the other – 'for balance', Mr Bolsover explained – was Peter Kropotkin, the Russian prince, sometime army officer and leader of scientific expeditions, whose growing anarchist convictions had led him to membership of a revolutionary party. This was followed by arrest, imprisonment in the Peter and Paul Fortress, escape and thirty years' exile, much of which he spent in England. The portraits were neatly labelled 'Salisbury' and 'Kropotkin', for the benefit, Cooper guessed, of Mr Bolsover's fellow councillors.

Cooper took this display of photographs as an expression of Mr Bolsover's unwillingness to be pigeonholed, a reproach to the other councillors with their party slogans and leaflets, and an attempt to baffle them by staking out the broadest possible political territory for himself. But despite the wide divergence in the two men's political views there were, arguably, areas of common ground. Both believed in strong social ties, treasured individual liberty and regarded the state with suspicion. It is always possible that Mr Bolsover was in fact attempting a synthesis of their views, announcing himself an unlikely and dangerously combustible mixture of anarchist and High Tory.

Cooper had come to think of the woods as his uncle's

natural habitat, and in this bare windowless office he looked as out of place as the coffee jar of spruce needles that he kept on the desk. But Mr Bolsover appeared quite at home, and he was as full of ideas as ever. On the day Cooper visited, he found him studying the illustrations in a biography of Gladstone.

'Has it ever occurred to you,' he said, 'that there are fashions in expressions, just as there are in clothes? Look at the expression on his face.' Cooper looked: it was a formal portrait of Gladstone, taken in the last decade of his life. 'Isn't it extraordinary? Hawkish and slightly distracted at the same time. You wouldn't see anyone with a face like that today.'

'I don't see why not.'

'You wouldn't. It's a typical late Victorian expression. Florence Nightingale used to do it as well. If you and I were to meet them today, the expressions on their faces would seem as outlandish as the way they dressed.'

Cooper suggested that it might have been a consequence of the long exposures needed in those days, and the effort of keeping the face set in a certain way for several seconds, or of the fact that the camera was still a relatively novel and perhaps unsettling piece of apparatus.

'I considered that,' his uncle said, 'but I don't think it can be either of those things. It's true for other periods as well, you see. I was looking at some pictures from the 1920s the other day, for example, and when people smiled in those days they used to show their teeth more than they do now. You can't put that down to a long exposure, or lack of familiarity with a camera. Charlie Chaplin used to do it, and he must have had his picture taken thousands of times.'

'But surely,' Cooper said, 'the human face can only make a certain number of expressions and everyone makes them all?'

'Yes, but we don't *read* all of them. At different times in history, people have responded to certain expressions and not to others. Our times dictate which expressions we read and which have meaning and which we respond to.'

'How can you prove that?'

'I'm afraid it's impossible to prove. The theory itself is only possible because of all these old photographs. We wouldn't have known about it at all otherwise, because we wouldn't have been able to see the faces of people who lived at different times. But I don't think I'm the first to suspect that people only read a fraction of each other's expressions. A few great communicators have probably been aware of it in every generation. I think Lloyd George knew, for example. I think that's why he grew a moustache.'

'What for?'

'To cultivate an area of mystery in the centre of his face, so that his expressions would be harder to read and also so that they wouldn't go out of date. And in fact when you see a picture of him today, his face looks remarkably contemporary. I expect it will in another hundred years as well. All because of the moustache.'

'So are you going to grow a moustache yourself?'

'No. Apart from anything else, a good one takes a lot of looking after. To have the right effect, a moustache must be substantial. If it's just a few bristles on the upper lip, you'll look shifty and indecisive. But it can't be too bushy either. It might be possible to get away with a wild shaggy beard, but a moustache has to be well kept. And that's the difficulty with my lifestyle. It's easy to keep a moustache indoors, in warm dry conditions. But it's damp in those woods – you've seen all the ferns and the moss on the tree trunks. That means two things. First, the hair grows twice as fast, so it has to be trimmed every day. That's a nuisance, but it's not an insurmountable problem. The real trouble is that the humidity makes the bristles curl, and the moustache loses its shape. So you have to dress it with wax, which is all right in fine weather, but as soon as you get a few drops of rain on it the whole thing comes unstuck. If it gets really wet the wax froths up, so it looks like you've been eating soap. And then who's going to listen to a word you say?'

'What about contemporary expressions, then?' Cooper said.

'This isn't a good age for expressions,' Mr Bolsover told him. 'There's too much visual stimulation, perhaps – people don't concentrate on a face in the way they used to. They only have the attention span to read very simple expressions. But there are a few that I think are characteristic of our times. There's one I've seen on your face quite often, for example.'

'What's that?'

'Impatience and contempt with a thin overlay of polite interest. There, you're doing it now.'

As a workplace Mr Bolsover's new office was unpromising – as Cooper said, if the council staff had deliberately set out to isolate him they could not have done much better. As it turned out, however, the small size of the office worked in his favour. There was room for a computer on the desk but no printer, so when he wanted to print something out or to use the photocopier he had to go along the corridor to one of the other offices. This gave him excellent opportunities to eavesdrop on the opposition.

As for the kitchen, it was no more inspiring than

the office. The hot tap dripped, and there were always tea-stained mugs on the draining board, crumbs on the worktop and a few dog-eared magazines on the table. But it became for Mr Bolsover what the House of Commons smoking room had been for Stanley Baldwin: the place where much of his real work was done. When he had a speech or an important vote to prepare for, Baldwin would sit all afternoon in the smoking room, making small talk with anyone who came in, reading the *Strand Magazine* or simply gazing into the middle distance, to the despair of his parliamentary aides. But he was not wasting time: he was working, assessing the general mood, putting out his tongue like a lizard to taste the air, the better to choose the right tone for his speech. In the same way Mr Bolsover spent hours in the kitchen next to his office, studying the agenda for forthcoming meetings, leafing through the pages of *Good Housekeeping* and *Woman's Own* and drinking cup after cup of spruce tea. He knew from past experience that everyone comes into the office kitchen sooner or later, and that if he stayed there for long enough he would meet them all.

In any case, the other councillors were keen to meet Mr Bolsover, and one by one they came to look for him in his office or in the kitchen, eager to get the measure of him. There was more to it than simple curiosity. The factions and rivalries of local government can be as bitter as any in Westminster, and they are only intensified by the small size of the battleground, as there is no getting away to one's constituency on the night train, and no overseas trips or international gatherings to lend a sense of perspective. In this environment an independent could play a useful role, not just as someone to be sounded out and co-opted for important votes, but also as a kind of safety valve, a focus for displays of forbearance and good-humoured banter which the cut-throat nature of local politics did not otherwise permit.

But Mr Bolsover confounded them from the start. With his patrician air as he offered them a cup of spruce tea, and the penetrating gaze he turned on them as they drank it, he was impossible to patronise. They were unnerved by their initial encounters with him, and to a man and a woman they went away uncertain whether they had found an ally or an opponent.

At that time the Conservatives were the largest group on the council, but no party had overall control. The voting was often close, and Mr Bolsover found that his support was eagerly solicited, a fact he proved to be ruthlessly effective at exploiting. On one occasion, when several Conservative members of the council were absent, he agreed to vote with Labour and the Liberal

Democrats to defeat a Conservative motion to transfer ownership of a recreation ground in Seaford from
the Borough Council to the local Parish Council. He
had lent his vote on the understanding that he would
receive backing in turn for a motion of support for the
troglodyte housing scheme which he had originally
outlined in the letters page of the *Sussex Journal*. It is a
testament to his powers of persuasion that he managed
to convince as many as three Liberal Democrats and a
Labour councillor to vote with him.

But activities of this kind counted for little in comparison with his public appearances. It is after all through
their speeches and interventions in debates that politicians capture the public imagination, not their skills in
the back office or the committee room, which are less
visible and whose effects are less immediately apparent.
Asquith's brisk efficiency in dealing with his boxes, or
Baldwin's uncanny ability to take the emotional temperature of a room, pale beside Disraeli's flashes of wit
on the floor of the House and the stirring cadences of
Churchill. In the same way Mr Bolsover's performance
at the next meeting of the full council, about a month
after his election, was far better remembered than any
of his other exploits during his time in office.

The meeting was scheduled to begin at seven o'clock,
but Cooper was late arriving and by the time he had

found a seat in the public gallery and examined his order paper the councillors were already well into item eleven, a debate on the council's priorities for the coming year.

'I felt in Councillor Granville's speech the lack of a strategic plan. You come up with initiatives, but I believe they are largely opportunistic. The aspiration to freeze council tax is admirable, but we are concerned about the amounts being spent on consultants and temporary staff. We are also concerned that the drive to cut spending will limit access to public services for some of the most vulnerable people in our community.'

'Hear, hear.'

'The paucity of funding for youth services is a case in point. And why is there such a massive underspend in the adult social care budget, when we hear from constituents that they are not able to access these services and have been told that they are not available due to lack of funding?'

Cooper had chosen a seat in the public gallery directly opposite where Mr Bolsover was sitting, and while the councillors were talking he watched his uncle closely. He was following the debate with lively attention, but his face gave no clue as to his reactions. From time to time he would scribble a note in the margin of his order paper.

Mr Bolsover had startled his fellow councillors, who

had been ready for him to appear in some outlandish
get-up, by arriving in the council chamber dressed in
a suit and tie. They did not know what an effort it had
cost him to achieve this. The morning after his election victory he had taken his suits and a selection of
ties from the bedroom cupboard at Barcombe Crescent
and hung them in a hollow tree near his camp, with a
piece of plastic sheeting to keep the bat droppings off
them. The night before the meeting he had sat by the
fire polishing his shoes to a brilliant shine, while the
owls hooted in the branches above his head.

'Councillor Stokes.'

'There is always a temptation in these debates to
respond point by point to what the last speaker has said.
I won't be tempted in that way, I will talk more generally. Now, I didn't intend to make a political speech. I
had thought of taking a more mellow approach, but as
one of my constituents said to me the other day, these
are difficult times, the country faces its worst economic
crisis for a generation, public disenchantment with politicians has never been greater – is this really the time
for you to be mellow, Graham? So I will say that I'm
slightly surprised by the speeches made by the leader of
the council and the leader of the so-called opposition
– who I have a great deal of respect for – those speeches
lacked warmth, they lacked vision ...'

To Cooper, watching from the gallery, the councillors resembled members of a strange club. How many of their constituents would recognise them if they passed them in the street? But they all knew each other. They had met here every month, in some cases for years on end, to subject each other to their plodding rhetoric, to snort derisively when their opponents were speaking, to make a show of examining their watches and yawning and rolling their eyes. Despite all this he felt a certain admiration for them. Here they were on a wet Wednesday night, talking essentially to themselves, while outside, beyond the thick velvet curtains, the rest of the town went on with its business.

'Councillor Bolsover.'

In this assembly, where the councillors were restricted to five minutes for their initial statements and three minutes for replies and subsequent questions, the scope for great oratory was limited. There was no place for the epic filibuster, no chance for a speaker to work up a head of steam, no need for him to fortify himself, as Gladstone had done during his longer speeches, with eggs beaten up in sherry. This was arguably a blessing, but it makes it more difficult to measure Mr Bolsover against the great parliamentary speakers of the past. The truth, I think, is that he was an effective orator rather than a great one. His manner as he rose to speak was collected and deliberate. His voice was not loud, but penetrating. It carried easily into the furthest corners of the room, even without the help of the microphone on his desk. Its curiously nasal quality lent a sardonic overtone to much of what he said.

'Mr Mayor, I'd like first of all to thank my constituents for electing me to this post and giving me the opportunity to address this meeting. But I must say I am dismayed by the manner in which business is conducted here. Our task is simply to make a number of basic decisions about administrative matters. Party politics have no bearing on issues such as the setting of library budgets or the enforcement of parking regulations, and yet all our discussions are dominated by political squabbles and posturing. I hear the rumble of national politics in the background of every exchange, like gunfire below the horizon. Some of my fellow councillors appear to think that if they shout loudly enough they will be heard in Parliament. But who is listening?' He waved in the direction of the public gallery. 'Look at all these empty seats.'

'Councillor, you're making a statement. Do you have a question?'

'Thank you, Mr Mayor. I'm just getting to it. The discussion so far has displayed a worrying lack of focus. We would do well to remember the warning of Lord

Salisbury, that our problems cannot be conjured away by the plentiful administration of platitudes and rose-water. If we stopped wasting our energy on these gro-tesque charades – '

'Your question, please, Councillor.'

'My question is for the leader of the council. Does he in fact have anything to offer my constituents apart from platitudes and rosewater?'

'Councillor Granville.'

The leader of the council might have been expected to deal tolerantly with a new councillor on his first out-ing in the council chamber. But Councillor Granville was not inclined to exercise restraint. He suspected, although he could not prove, that the time-honoured graffiti which had recently appeared on the hand dryer in the men's lavatory outside the council chamber ('Place hands under dryer to hear a short speech by Councillor Granville') was the work of Mr Bolsover.

'Thank you for your question, Councillor. It's always good to hear a new voice in the council chamber. But I fear that living under a hedge and subsisting on a diet of berries and rainwater may have eroded Councillor Bolsover's grip on reality.'

The other councillors, who had remained silent throughout Mr Bolsover's speech, greeted this remark with hearty laughter.

'In fact, this administration can be proud of its record over the last few years, and I have no objection to reviewing some of the highlights for Councillor Bolsover's benefit. We have continued to improve social care services, while cutting waste. We have approved more affordable housing developments over the past three years than the previous administration managed in eight years. And last year we embarked on a road improvement programme which has been a great success, with fifteen thousand potholes filled and forty miles of road completely resurfaced in the twelve months to April.'

'Humbug!' cried Mr Bolsover, waving his order paper.

But Councillor Granville ploughed on. 'Looking to the future, we are committed to continuing these programmes. In difficult economic times our priority must be to focus on using our limited funds effectively. Nevertheless, this year we intend to bring forward several exciting initiatives, such as a drive to improve community safety, which will see the introduction of new street lighting and traffic calming measures ...'

By now many of the councillors were starting to droop in their seats and to smother genuine yawns. One man kept blowing out his cheeks, with weariness, Cooper thought, rather than exasperation, and he noticed a woman crouching behind her desk and surreptitiously bolting the remains of her packed lunch.

Mr Bolsover, too, was crouching behind his desk. From this angle Cooper could not see clearly what he was doing, but he appeared to be pulling at something under his seat. After a few seconds he straightened up again and sat listening to Councillor Granville with an air of intense absorption.

Cooper himself was struggling to maintain his concentration, and reflecting that the councillors' voices sounded like water running into a bath, when he became aware of a disturbance on Mr Bolsover's side of the chamber. There was a scuffling along the rows of seats, little shrieks and gasps of surprise, and people were craning their heads to look under the desks.

As the disturbance came from the opposition benches, Councillor Granville perhaps assumed that it was a deliberate attempt to distract him. He went on speaking.

'I would also like to mention social care services, which we have sorted out – ten years ago they were in a mess. It was our administration which brought the funding under control ...'

He faltered. A stocky creature about the size of a small dog had emerged from the end of a row of seats and was making its way up the aisle. But it was not a dog. It had a silvery coat, and black-and-white stripes on its head.

'A badger!' said Councillor Stokes excitedly. 'It's a badger!'

When it came to the open space in front of the mayor's desk the badger stopped and looked around, as if uncertain where to go next.

'Mr Mayor,' said Councillor Granville, with a rather forced attempt at jauntiness, 'we seem to have a visitor.'

'Councillor Bolsover, do you know anything about this animal?' the mayor asked.

'What animal?' Mr Bolsover's expression was impassive.

Before the mayor could answer there was an indignant shout from the councillor who sat immediately behind Mr Bolsover.

'Look what was under his chair!' She had ducked under the desk and reappeared holding a cat basket and a large piece of sacking, which she held aloft for everyone to see.

'Councillor Bolsover,' said the mayor, 'please leave the chamber.'

Cooper looked nervously down at his uncle, expecting an outburst of righteous indignation. But none came. Mr Bolsover simply rose to his feet, swung his legs over his desk and stalked out of the room.

As the door closed behind him the badger, evidently having made up its mind, bolted with surprising speed back along the aisle and plunged beneath the first row of seats on the other side. Its claws clattered on the wooden floor as it ran along the row, and the councillors jumped out of their seats. Several of them clambered onto their desks or stood on their chairs.

'It's pissed all over my order paper,' someone cried.

'It's chewed a hole in my handbag.'

At the end of the row the badger emerged, paused, caught Councillor Granville's eye for a second and then turned and ran back the other way, under the second row of seats.

By now the room was in uproar. The mayor banged his gavel on the desk. 'The meeting is suspended,' he announced, shouting to be heard above the noise. 'Clear the chamber.'

The mayor collected his papers and left the room, followed by his deputy carrying the mace, while the councillors hurriedly gathered up their coats and bags and made in a body for the exit. A few minutes later they crowded into the public gallery to watch as the deputy and a security guard returned to begin the tricky task of recapturing the badger, which had gone to ground under a stack of chairs.

'Did you know that badgers have the most powerful

bite of any animal?' said the councillor next to Cooper. 'Worse than an alligator. I wouldn't go near it.'

'It's a health risk,' added Councillor Stokes, who was standing on the other side of him. 'Probably riddled with tuberculosis.'

But the security guard and the deputy were both armed with mops, which they had taken from the broom cupboard in the corridor outside. They goaded the badger from its hiding place by rattling their mops against the chair legs and chased it twice round the chamber before they managed to get it out of the door, which the mayor held open for them. Then they drove it down the corridor and shut it in the broom cupboard. The security guard went to call the animal shelter, and the councillors trooped back downstairs and resumed their seats. The deputy fetched the mace, and the meeting continued. But Cooper did not stay to watch any more of it. He hurried outside in search of his uncle.

7

Triumph and Disaster

A brief report of Mr Bolsover's activities at the council meeting appeared in the next edition of the *Sussex Journal*:

> Councillor Bolsover, representing Winterbourne ward, was expelled from a meeting of Lewes Borough Council on Wednesday night after a live badger was found in the council chamber.
>
> The animal was quickly recaptured by council security staff and safely released back into the wild, with the assistance of experts from the local animal shelter. A piece of sacking and a cat basket, in which the animal is believed to have been transported, were later found under Councillor Bolsover's seat.
>
> In a statement the leader of the Borough Council,

Michael Granville, labelled the action 'reckless and disgraceful'.

Councillor Bolsover was not available for comment.

The newspaper report had been written by Mr Tilling. It was a truncated version of a far longer and more dramatic account provided by Cooper. There was no further press coverage, a fact that would have been less remarkable if Mr Bolsover's career until that point had not received so much attention. As a rule the local papers took little interest in the activities of borough councillors, and although at every council meeting a number of seats were reserved for the press, it was seldom that anyone sat in them. As a mysterious firebrand living in the woods Mr Bolsover had constituted a story. But his reinvention as a local councillor with an office and a schedule of regular public appearances had stripped him of much of his mystique, and he dropped out of the news as swiftly as he had entered it. The news channels and the national press were distracted by the latest convulsions in the Eurozone, the local papers had turned their attention to the row over proposals for a waste-processing facility in Uckfield, and his erstwhile champion Professor Berceau was in Caracas, making a documentary about the origins of Latin American revolutionary movements.

In his report, Mr Tilling did not apportion responsibility or a motive for the disruption to the meeting, but let the circumstantial evidence speak for itself. The councillors were in no doubt that Mr Bolsover had released the badger in an act of premeditated and deliberate disruption. Cooper himself was not so sure. Leaving the council offices on the night in question, he had found his uncle sitting on a bench across the road from the entrance. Mr Bolsover explained that he had found the badger a few weeks earlier with a broken leg by the side of the road and taken it to the vet, who had set the leg and put a splint on it. Since then he had been looking after it himself.

'Don't you need some kind of qualification for that?' Cooper asked him.

'I know what I'm doing.'

The animal had recovered well from its injury. Immediately before the meeting, he had taken it back to the vet for a final check-up and to have the splint removed, and he had come directly from the vet's surgery to the council chamber. He had been planning to release the badger into the woods later that night. He had not meant it to escape during the meeting.

'But I saw you fiddling with the cage just before it got out.'

'I was checking to see if I'd fastened it properly.'

Cooper was not convinced by this explanation. He could not think of any more plausible way in which Mr Bolsover might have acquired the badger, and it was just possible that his reason for bringing it with him to the meeting had been perfectly innocent. But he could not believe that it had got out by accident: the timing was too much to ask of coincidence. Mr Bolsover had had a motive for disrupting the meeting, and on the impulse of the moment he had acted using the means to hand.

Whatever his standing in the chamber, Mr Bolsover's commitment to his office was unwavering. Few of the other councillors held surgeries these days, finding that their constituents preferred to communicate by email, but Mr Bolsover was determined to meet his in person. He booked the church hall in Highdown Road for this purpose, and made himself available at 7 p.m. on alternate Wednesdays and at 3 p.m. on the last Saturday of every month.

At first the people of Winterbourne ward were as eager to meet him as his fellow councillors had been, and his initial surgery was well attended. A crowd of twenty or thirty gathered outside the church hall that evening and waited for him to appear. They were not disappointed. At two minutes before seven he arrived, carrying a briefcase, and wearing on his head an enormous fur hat with earflaps in the Russian style but visibly misshapen and unevenly stitched. It was made of genuine rabbit fur, as he explained to Cooper afterwards.

'I cured the skins myself. Shot the rabbits too, there are hundreds of them on the railway embankment.'

'I didn't know you had a gun.'

'A catapult, actually. It's easy enough. Go out there in the evening when they're feeding, lie down behind a bush, let them get used to you, then take aim at the nearest one and put a ball bearing through its head at five yards.'

'A ball bearing?'

'Or a marble,' his uncle said quickly, 'or a stone, even – there are plenty of those lying around.'

But the mystery of Cooper's bicycle was solved. Those ball bearings had been extracted from the bottom bracket, wiped clean of grease, and then catapulted into the brains of the local rabbits.

'I did that every night for a week or so, but after a while the rabbits got fed up with being shot at. They're not as stupid as they look, you know. In the end they wouldn't come out at all when I was around, even when I was lying behind a bush. That's why the two at the edge here are a bit threadbare. They came off the road.'

Mr Bolsover shook hands gravely with everyone and thanked them for coming. They followed him inside and made themselves as comfortable as they could on the hard wooden chairs, watching with interest as he opened his briefcase and took out a camping stove, a small kettle, and a paper bag of spruce needles. He filled the kettle at the kitchen tap, lit the stove and brewed up on the front step. Then he handed round the tea in a single china mug from the kitchen while they told him their problems.

As it turned out, this did not take very long. Many of those present were constituents who had not met him on the doorstep or voted for him and had come now simply because they were curious to see their new councillor in person. They went away satisfied, leaving Mr Bolsover to deal with a man unhappy with the slow progress of a planning application, a couple from the board of the Winterbourne Youth Centre whose lease was coming up for renewal and who were worried that the council would put up the rent, and a deputation from the 4th Lewes Sea Scouts who wanted him to address them on the subject of knots.

After that first meeting, the attendance at Mr Bolsover's surgeries quickly declined. Soon he counted it a busy evening if he had seen three or four people, and sometimes nobody came at all. He dealt as well as he could with their problems, with boundary disputes and planning appeals and complaints about the frequency of bin collections, but many were not strictly within the remit of a local councillor. He was consulted for gardening tips and advice on job applications, and on one occasion he was asked to help find a missing tortoise-shell cat.

'And half the time,' he told Cooper, 'they don't seem to expect me to do anything at all – I think they just want someone to talk to.'

For both parties it was often an exercise in disappointment. Mr Bolsover made no attempt to disguise his impatience with what he considered foolish demands on his time, and even when he was in a more tolerant mood he would invariably steer the conversation from the matter at hand to a more general discussion of politics. He was not like the zealot patiently repeating a party line but a more disconcerting proposition, one who genuinely relished the debate. Then he resembled a terrier, stocky and pugnacious, his head on one side, eyes glinting ferociously under the wiry eyebrows, seizing a topic in his teeth like an old slipper, worrying at it and refusing to let go. His constituents reacted with bewilderment and frank alarm, as though he might be about to jump over the table and bite their ankles. They seldom came back.

As they discovered during the surgeries, and as Cooper knew from his own experience, Mr Bolsover could be difficult company, impatient and dismissive, and it might be asked why someone with such apparently misanthropic tendencies would have exposed himself to public scrutiny in this way. But a misanthrope is one with a low opinion of humanity, whereas I think Mr Bolsover's trouble was rather that he expected too much of his fellow citizens, and was then doomed to be disappointed.

During the election campaign Cooper had seen his uncle nearly every day. Since the election, Mr Bolsover had been occupied with council business, and they met far less frequently. Cooper was not unduly surprised to have seen nothing of him for several weeks after the night of his expulsion from the council chamber. But when his uncle failed to appear at the next council meeting (Cooper sat in the public gallery all evening, in full view of his uncle's empty seat) he became concerned, and decided the next Saturday morning to go out and look for him.

It had been months since his last visit to the woods. Now the trees were in full leaf, brambles and nettles had grown up along the paths and the clearings were choked with bracken. But he found his way back to the camp without difficulty. As he got closer he could smell woodsmoke, and when he reached the top of the bank and looked down into the hollow he saw everything more or less as it had been before. The tarpaulin had gone, but the fire was alight, and on the trivet a pan of water was just coming to the boil. Only Mr Bolsover was nowhere to be seen. Cooper called out a few times, but there was no answer.

He climbed down the bank and sat on one of the logs by the fire. It was very peaceful. Somewhere nearby two wood pigeons were calling to each other and there was a smell of damp earth and leaf mould. In the distance he could hear the sound of a train going past. Soon the water was boiling fiercely, rattling the lid of the pan, and Cooper thought he might as well make himself some tea and wait for his uncle to return. He opened the trunk where the tea things were kept and took out the teapot and caddy. Then he measured out the tea, took the lid off the pan and scooped water into the pot. There was no milk for the tea, but he found half a lemon in the trunk and decided to use that instead.

'Pour me a cup too, would you?'

The voice of Mr Bolsover came from just behind him, but when Cooper turned round there was nobody there. The bank at this point was about ten feet high, steep and sandy, a tangle of exposed tree roots and trailing ivy and periwinkle. It would have been impossible for anyone to climb down it and up again so quickly without being heard, and Cooper guessed that his uncle had concealed himself in the undergrowth at the top.

'Why don't you come down and pour it yourself?' he shouted. There was no answer. Cooper went across to the other side of the hollow where the ground sloped more gently, climbed out and walked round to the top of the bank. He looked all round the clump of fir trees, but there was nobody there. Puzzled, he went back the way he had come, and as he made his way down into the hollow he found Mr Bolsover sitting by the fire, cutting the lemon into slices with his penknife. He was so pleased and excited by the success of his trick that he was having difficulty slicing it straight.

'Lemon in your tea?' he asked.

'All right, where were you hiding?'

'Do you want me to show you? Sit down on that log.' He went over to the foot of the bank, where the ivy was thickest. 'Don't look round till I tell you.'

Cooper sat down obediently and gazed into the fire. Behind him there was a brief scrabbling and rustling and then, sounding slightly out of breath, his uncle's voice said, 'OK, you can look now.' But Cooper did not want to seem too eager. He drank his tea and poked the fire, and when he finally did turn round, Mr Bolsover had disappeared. He got up and examined the tree roots and the tangled mass of ivy at the foot of the bank, then backed off a few paces to scan the undergrowth at the top, but he could see no trace of his uncle. He was on the point of giving up when he heard a snort of exasperation from within the bank, and a hand appeared between the tree roots and waved. It drew aside the curtain of ivy to reveal a triangular opening between the roots that was just big enough to crawl through. The hand withdrew, and Cooper bent down and stuck his head through the entrance.

Inside, the bank had been hollowed out to create a dry, sandy-walled chamber about eight feet deep and five feet high, with the exposed tree roots acting as natural pit props. It made Cooper think of a sleeping compartment on a train. On one side there was a narrow bed covered with blankets, and on the other a low bench running the length of the wall. Both of these items were made from offcuts of wood. Beneath them there was a floor of rough boards, which on closer inspection Cooper recognised as one of the missing sections from his parents' back fence.

Mr Bolsover was sitting on the bed, lighting a candle lamp. He closed the glass door carefully and hung it up on a hook that had been screwed into a root directly above his head. 'Well,' he said, 'come in, if you're coming in.'

Cooper crawled inside and sat down on the bench. The lamp was still swinging about, and threw odd flickering shadows across the walls.

'How do you like my bolt-hole?' he asked.

Seen from inside, without the ivy to obscure it, the structure of the entrance was clear. A thick horizontal root formed the threshold. Immediately behind it a low door frame, made of three stout posts, had been wedged in place. The door itself was made of plywood reinforced on the inside with battens, and opened inwards. Around the entrance there were various gaps and chinks which let the light in.

'What happened to the tarpaulin?' Cooper asked.

'The old arrangement wasn't very practical,' said Mr Bolsover. 'I knew that if I was going to stay here for any length of time I'd need something more permanent. More weatherproof, and more discreet. A place to hide from unwelcome visitors.'

'Do you get many?'

'There's always someone,' he said. 'Ramblers, people on horses, boys on farting motorbikes. Farmers. And soon after I got here I was down at the bottom of the hill collecting firewood and I ran into a man wearing wellington boots and carrying a clipboard. He asked me what I was doing and I said I was out for a walk, and I asked him what he was doing and he said he was monitoring the bat population. But of course I had a whole lot of sticks under my arm, and he looked at the sticks and asked me if I was planning to start a fire. I said I wasn't (which was quite true, by the way, because I'd already lit one) and he said he hoped not, because lighting fires was strictly against National Trust by-laws. I said, well of course I wouldn't want to do anything that contravened National Trust by-laws, and he looked at me again suspiciously and went away. But after that I realised that if I was going to stay here much longer I'd have to go underground.

'I had to keep it a secret, of course. I could only dig in the evenings, when there was no one about. Then before it got too dark I'd cart away all the sand I'd dug out and spread it about a bit and cover it with leaf mould, so nobody could see what I'd been doing. That's why it took so long. But the work itself was surprisingly easy. This bank is so soft, it's like digging into a snowdrift. And it got easier as it went along.

'It's not my choice, you know,' he went on. 'I'd have been quite happy with a little cabin – I could cut down some saplings for the frame, get some old bricks and put up a chimney … But they won't let you live in cabins in the woods these days, so I had to do this instead.'

'They won't let you dig bunkers either.'

'Maybe not, but the difference is that no one can see I've done it. The best way to hold territory is for no one to know that you hold it. I forget who said that – I think it was von Clausewitz.'

The last few times Cooper had seen his uncle, it had been across the council chamber. Now, sitting with him in this space so confined that their knees were touching, he could not help observing that there had been changes in Mr Bolsover's physical appearance. For one thing, he had become more thickset. His shoulders were broader than Cooper remembered them ever being before, and his arms too were surprisingly well developed, like those of a mole or some other burrowing creature. And when his uncle sat up into the candlelight, Cooper's eyes were drawn to the open neck of his shirt, where a thick mat of hair was visible. He had never been a particularly hairy man, but this was a dense, luxuriant growth – he wondered how he had not noticed it before. There were also vigorous tufts of hair protruding from his shirt cuffs.

These details made me uneasy. It is at points like this in a life where there is so little on the official record that the biographer relies all the more on the testimony of sober and credible witnesses. And it is exactly here that I began to have misgivings about the reliability of Cooper's account.

'What did you use for digging?'

'This.' Mr Bolsover held up a trowel, the worn edge of which gleamed in the candlelight. 'Of course, you can't dig wherever you like because of all these roots, but there's no danger of the roof falling in.'

Cooper leant back against the wall of the chamber. It was surprisingly comfortable. A shallow alcove supported his back like a bucket chair, and about halfway down there was a small lump of root that rubbed agreeably between his shoulder blades. The back of the chamber was covered with a great network of roots, and in the niches between them – he saw, as his eyes grew accustomed to the lamplight – various items had been wedged: an alarm clock, a box of candles, a toothbrush in a glass, and even a short length of shelving on which a row of books had been arranged.

'I'm thinking of expanding, actually,' said Mr Bolsover. 'I want to put a fireplace in here. I haven't lit the fire so often recently – I don't feel the cold as much as I used to – but I'll need it in the winter. Did you see the big fir tree on the top of the bank? Well, if you dug straight up for about three feet from where you're sitting now, you'd come out just underneath it. There'll be a retractable chimney pipe, and when I light the fire in the evenings I'll extend the chimney into the branches, so all the smoke gets carried into the top of the fir tree and blows away. No one will know I've got a fire going in here, even if they walk right past me.'

He outlined his plans for further earthworks; a roomier dugout, storage chambers for firewood, and a well so that he would not have to fetch water from the middle of the field.

'And a root cellar,' he said, 'which I've already dug. That reminds me – I need to show you something.' He led Cooper out of the dugout and a little further along the bank, where he lifted aside the trailing ivy to reveal the root cellar. Like his dugout, it was cut into the side of the bank, but it was a much smaller chamber with a low roof and a floor of loose sand. He reached inside and pulled out a long narrow cardboard box, which he laid carefully on the ground. Inside, neatly packed, there were about a dozen rockets.

'I've been thinking that I need some way of communicating in an emergency,' he explained, 'and this is it.'

'What kind of emergency?'

'Oh, you know the sort of thing. A broken leg. Frostbite. A forest fire, perhaps.'

'Who are you going to communicate with?'

'With you, of course.' He took four rockets out of the box, stuck one in the ground and wrapped the others in a bin liner before handing them to Cooper.

'Isn't that what mobile phones are for?'

'I can't recharge the battery out here. And anyway the

reception's very poor.' He closed the box and replaced it carefully in the root cellar, pulling the ivy back across the opening.

'Now,' he said, 'if I need to get in touch with you I'll let off a rocket from the edge of the wood at a certain time – let's say at dusk. You'll be able to see it from the back of the house, and when you do, you fire one of your rockets to let me know you've seen my signal. Then we'll rendezvous at the edge of the wood, by the stile. Can you remember that?'

'Yes, I think so.'

'Good. Then let's try it.' He pulled up the rocket he had stuck in the ground. 'You go back home now, and I'll fire this in about half an hour. Then when you see it, you fire one of yours. You need to stick it in a nice soft bit of ground – your vegetable bed will do.'

Cooper returned home with the bundle of fireworks under his arm. A few minutes after he arrived back at the house, a rocket shot up from behind the hill into the darkening sky and exploded in a shower of green sparks. At this distance the sound of the explosion itself was lost. Suddenly excited despite himself, Cooper stuck one of his own rockets into the earth between two rows of broad beans and lit the fuse. It burst above the back gardens with a muffled crack, much quieter than he had expected. Then he hurried back out of the garden gate and over the hills to the stile by the wood, where he found his uncle pacing up and down.

'You took your time,' he said, looking at his watch. 'But it worked. Keep the rest of those rockets in the shed, and don't let them get damp.'

Unless they have the open-ended mandate of the revolutionary vanguard or the president for life, most politicians have a limited period in which to make good. Mr Bolsover's time was more limited than most, because the regular council elections were scheduled to take place less than a year after his by-election victory, and along with all the other councillors he would have to contest his seat again.

A brief term in office need not be a barrier to getting things done, and given the right conditions it is possible to accomplish a great deal. Lord Salisbury's first minority government of 1885 held office for barely seven months, but in that time he was still able to see a number of important bills through Parliament, while his foreign policy was distinguished by the successful handling of the Bulgarian crisis. Mr Bolsover of course had two further constraints to contend with. He had little influence – he was a single voice in the council chamber – and he was operating through the mechanism of local rather than national government.

By any measure his achievements were profoundly limited. In addition to the vote on his affordable housing scheme, he proposed a motion that all council meetings should be held outdoors, in the castle precincts or in the Eastgate Wharf car park behind the High Street, 'where the councillors will be more visible to the public and the quality of their decisions will be improved by the invigorating effects of the fresh air'. On another occasion he moved that the council should consolidate and extend its powers, 'freeing ourselves', as he put it, 'from the dead hand of central government control and the impositions of the County Council. Why not model ourselves on the great city-states of the past, on Athens and Florence? We should demand full municipal control of all our affairs, except perhaps defence and foreign policy.' None of these motions was passed, but he did score one modest success. In exchange for his vote on a motion to introduce a twenty-mile-per-hour speed limit outside schools, Mr Bolsover had managed to persuade the Planning Committee to approve an extension to the lease of the youth centre in his ward with no increase in the rent. On the other hand, as Cooper pointed out, he might equally well have campaigned for this outcome without being in office at all.

As for public opinion, there are no approval ratings for borough councillors, as there are for presidents of the United States. But judging by the reactions of most of his constituents after they had attended his surgeries they would probably have been at the lower end of the range, closer to those of, say, Richard Nixon in 1974 than Franklin D. Roosevelt in 1945.

In these circumstances it came as a surprise to Cooper when Mr Bolsover chose to stand for election again. But this time round he was not simply campaigning for another four years in office, as Cooper understood when he read the campaign literature. His leaflets were stuffed through doors and posted on telegraph poles and the walls of bus shelters, on telephone exchange boxes and on the boarded-up windows of empty shops, not just in the ward where Mr Bolsover was standing but right across the district. They bore a closely printed communication which was part manifesto, part polemic and part call to action. This was the text:

Barely one in three eligible voters turned out at the last council election. I mention this not as a criticism but to illustrate a point. It seems idle to present a manifesto and ask for votes, when most of the electorate is considering not whom to vote for but whether to vote at all. And given that whichever way you vote, you are guaranteed another four years of political posturing and empty verbiage, this is entirely understandable.

Allow me instead to set out the nature of the problem as I see it. The first great mistake everyone makes these days is to treat politics as a full-time occupation. But it does not have to be like this. It never used to be. The Victorian prime ministers all had outside interests. Think of Disraeli with his novels, or Gladstone with his high moral purpose, as exemplified in the affair of Lady Lincoln. It was in this episode, I would argue, and not his first budget of 1853, or his defence of the Home Rule bills, that Gladstone's greatness was most readily apparent. In July 1849 Lady Lincoln, the wife of his old friend the Duke of Hamilton, had run away with Lord Walpole, and Gladstone took it upon himself to persuade her to return to her husband. He pursued the couple as far as Italy, at one point disguising himself as a mandolin player in order to gain access to their villa in Como. The mission was ultimately unsuccessful, as he never managed to confront Lady Lincoln, let alone convince her of the error of her ways. But it demonstrates Gladstone's most distinctive and admirable qualities: his restless energy, his readiness to embrace lost causes and his disregard for convention, coupled with an unwavering high-mindedness. At that time he had been a member of Parliament for sixteen years and had five young children (his wife was expecting a sixth). Which of today's politicians would put aside the demands of work and family to devote themselves to such a quixotic enterprise or, having embarked on it, have the determination to pursue it so far?

Neville Chamberlain provides another inspiring example of the pursuit of outside interests, less extreme than Gladstone's adventure, but just as unthinkable today. In 1933, when he was serving as Chancellor of the Exchequer, Chamberlain wrote a letter to *The Times* not about inflationary pressures or the benefits of leaving the gold standard, but about a grey wagtail that he had seen in St James's Park, 'running about on the now temporarily dry bed of the lake, near the dam below the bridge, and occasionally picking small insects out of the cracks in the dam'. Again, imagine the howls of outrage that would be raised if the current Chancellor admitted to having taken his mind off the size of the deficit for five minutes in order to study wagtails.

Today's politicians may not be willing to admit the fact, or they may not be aware of it, but dealing with affairs of state is quite a simple matter. There is no reason for it to be a profession. It should be an amateur pursuit, like bee-keeping. Politicians simply need to have the confidence to make decisions, and when they make them they will be better informed, because in between they will have taken the time to think their own thoughts and watch the grass grow.

The second great scourge of politics in our time is a preoccupation with appearances. This is directly related to the first problem. The more time politicians spend on parliamentary business, in the company of other politicians, the more anxious they become to give the impression of being normal and approachable. It was insecurities of this kind that lay behind the unedifying spectacle a few years back of a prime minister inviting the press to see him and his chancellor watching a football match on television, exchanging unconvincing badinage, munching pizza and sipping beer from the can, in a forlorn attempt to persuade the public that they were – contrary to all appearances – normal people. 'But you are politicians,' I want to cry. 'It is not your place to be normal.' Even if you did actually enjoy watching football, the voters would never accept it. You would deprive them of the very real pleasure of complaining that politicians are out of touch, that they live in ivory towers, that they do not understand the lives of ordinary people Far better to forget the football and confess to a passionate interest in ferrets, or croquet, or mud-wrestling, and defy the voters to reject you. They will appreciate your strength of character, if nothing else.

So I come to the subject of my campaign. The logic of my argument so far suggests that I should stand for election on a promise to be both unprofessional and unapproachable. But this time round I think that more drastic action is necessary.

What I propose is this. I offer myself as your candidate in next Thursday's election, but I urge you not to vote for me or for anyone else. Instead, I invite you to pack a small bag with a few essentials and join me on the summit of Malling Hill. Our presence in this prominent place, visible from all over the town, will communicate in a very public fashion our dissatisfaction with the manner in which our political affairs are run. We will also be able to exchange ideas about the kind of polity we want to see. Meanwhile, the everyday life of the borough will be suspended and we will bring about a productive hiatus in which our would-be representatives will be forced to come to terms. We will then have the opportunity to establish a new kind of political culture which will reinvigorate our democracy.

Vote with your feet! The tigers of wrath are wiser than the horses of instruction.

Mr Bolsover's mood during the campaign was altogether difficult to gauge. He did not have the energy that had carried him through his first campaign, but he was far from despairing. One morning he and Cooper went out to put up some posters, and on their way back they passed a primary school. Mr Bolsover stopped by the gate and peered through the bars. It was break time, and the children were capering about in the playground.

'We should give the vote to the under-tens,' he said. 'Look at these children – they've still got the right attitude. Their heads haven't been turned by petty distractions like holding down a job and paying the rent and raising a family. I know they'd vote for me if they had the chance. By the time they get to eighteen they're no longer capable of making a sensible political choice.'

On the morning of the election Cooper went to cast his vote. Apart from the election officials he was the only person in the polling station. On his way in to the office he had a clear view of Malling Hill above the rooftops. Except for a flock of sheep, the summit was bare, and as he passed through Winterbourne ward, where his uncle was standing, he noticed that the polling stations were packed, with queues extending out of the doors. The outlook for Mr Bolsover's campaign was not good. He wondered how many of the voters had read his uncle's closely printed broadsheet. Even if they were voting for him – which seemed unlikely – they would be going against his direct instructions.

The count that night for Winterbourne ward was virtually a private affair. Cooper was the only journalist present, and when he arrived he was not surprised to see that there was no sign of Mr Bolsover. Due to the increased turnout, it took much longer to count the ballot papers than before, and the count was not completed until well after midnight. When the time came for the candidates to assemble for the announcement of the results, Mr Bolsover was still nowhere to be found. Cooper guessed that he was maintaining his lonely vigil on the summit of Malling Hill, and as the returning officer read out the results he reflected that it was just as well. A total of 2,331 votes had been cast. This equated to a turnout of more than seventy per cent – remarkably high for a local election. The winning candidate had received 1,748 votes, while Mr Bolsover had polled 23 votes. It was, as the returning officer pointed out, a record swing against the incumbent.

Mr Bolsover's reaction was not long in coming. The morning after the election, a note was found pinned to the door of the Borough Council offices. It read simply: 'I have decided to resort to alternative measures.'

8

Days of Rage

Mr Bolsover was now facing one of the greatest tests in any political career: the moment of leaving office. After a lifetime devoted to attaining and exercising power, politicians frequently find themselves unprepared when it comes to giving it up, and they deal with the challenge in a variety of ways. Gladstone describes in his diaries (Volume 13) how after resigning as prime minister for the last time, he returned home to finish his translation of the *Odes* of Horace. 'The rest of my life will be holidays,' Churchill remarked sadly, on hearing the news that he had lost the 1945 general election, but shortly afterwards he began writing his history of the Second World War in six volumes. And John Major, after his election defeat in 1997, went in the morning to Buckingham Palace to resign and in the afternoon to the Oval to watch a cricket match (the Combined Universities against Surrey, according to his memoirs).

One evening a few days after the election Cooper was in the kitchen washing up when he heard a noise outside the back door. He guessed it was the hedgehog; he had put some food out for it the previous evening at about this time. But when he went to open the door he found his uncle there.

Mr Bolsover eyed the tin in Cooper's hand with some suspicion.

'What's that you've got there?'

'Cat food.'

'Have you got anything else to eat? I'm starving – I haven't eaten anything since lunch.'

There was no bread left, but Cooper found a malt loaf in the cupboard, and he brought it out and cut a couple of slices. He watched his uncle warily as he ate, looking for some insight into his state of mind.

'I suppose you're wondering why I didn't join you,' he said at last.

'Oh, I didn't expect you to join me,' said Mr Bolsover, and Cooper found this casual dismissal more wounding than a direct reproach.

'I was reporting the election.'

'Of course you were.'

He was in an oddly elated mood, and he would not

listen to Cooper's attempts to commiserate over the defeat.

'There's no need to be sorry,' he said. 'It was a triumph, in a way.'

'In what way?'

'The turnout was seventy-two per cent,' he said. 'That's a record. None of the other wards even managed fifty per cent.'

'Doesn't that make it worse?'

'Not at all,' he said. 'I've regained some of my faith in the electorate. The fact that they voted is the important thing. Who they voted for is really beside the point.'

What struck Cooper about his uncle's conversation that night was how little it corresponded to his expectations of a defeated political candidate. Certainly he recounted the difficulties of the campaign, what had gone wrong, but all in a curiously light-hearted way. He was remarkably unperturbed by the defeat, as if it had happened to somebody else. He insisted that his political career had not come to an end; rather, it had entered a new phase. He observed, mysteriously, that a tactical defeat could lead to a strategic victory. He spoke of 'redrawing the boundaries of my constituency'. He would no longer presume to represent anyone else, he said: from now on, he would represent only himself.

'Will you be all right?' Cooper asked him at last.

'I'll be fine.'

He cut up the rest of the malt loaf and spread the slices thickly with butter. Then he stood up, crammed one slice into his mouth and the others into his coat pocket, and went out into the night.

In the weeks that followed his fall from power, it might have been expected that Mr Bolsover would fade from public consciousness. But far from being forgotten, he was more present in the public mind than ever.

This became apparent when his name was linked to an epidemic of exploding parking meters, a type of vandalism for which Lewes has been notorious in recent years, ever since the council introduced widely resented parking restrictions and charges. Most of the incidents so far had involved the jamming of lit fireworks into the slots of the parking meters. But in the latest outbreak more powerful and destructive explosive charges had been used. It was widely believed that Mr Bolsover had been responsible for the explosions, and that they were the first example of the 'alternative measures' he had promised. Cooper was not so sure: as he pointed out, his uncle had never spoken out against parking charges during his time in office.

The smell of rotten eggs which hung over Lewes, as it did over much of Kent and Sussex, one Wednesday later that month was also attributed by many to the machinations of Mr Bolsover. Even after it was announced on the evening news that the source of the smell was in fact a leak from a chemical plant across the Channel, on the outskirts of Le Havre, the belief persisted that it had been an example of 'propaganda of the deed' on the part of Mr Bolsover. What exactly it was supposed to signify nobody could agree on, but as an illustration of the change in public attitudes to him since his election defeat, the episode is instructive.

Given that many of those spreading these rumours must have turned out only a few weeks earlier to eject him from office, his enduring hold on the collective imagination is remarkable. I can only conclude that some of the public dissatisfaction with him stemmed from the fact that, once elected, he lost the aura that had drawn the voters to him in the first place. Evidently Mr Bolsover in defeat was able to answer needs he could not have answered while in office.

The fascination that Mr Bolsover continued to exert is vividly illustrated by the story of his visit to a local restaurant, the Garden House. One afternoon the manager of that establishment had received a phone call, announcing that Mr Bolsover wanted a change from berries and rainwater and had decided to take himself out to lunch. He would be coming on the following Tuesday.

The news spread quickly. Lunch was served from midday, and although the restaurant was usually fairly quiet on a weekday lunchtime, by twelve-thirty on the appointed day it was filling up with people hoping to see Mr Bolsover at close quarters. Several reporters were present, and shortly before one o'clock a policeman walked in and sat down at a table in the corner. The appearance of a man in uniform provided a welcome distraction, and someone asked him if he'd come to arrest Mr Bolsover. But the policeman merely frowned and began to study his menu.

By now there was only one table still vacant: a table for two in the middle of the dining room, with a 'Reserved' sign on it. All eyes turned to this table: would Mr Bolsover come and claim it? The atmosphere was tense. And when at last two old ladies came in and were shown to the table by a waiter, they were met with angry and reproachful looks from the other diners, as if they were personally responsible for Mr Bolsover's failure to appear.

After this, a feeling of anticlimax settled over the restaurant. People started to mutter that it wasn't surprising Mr Bolsover hadn't turned up, with all these reporters waiting for him and a policeman as well. By two-thirty most had paid their bills and left, and at three o'clock when the restaurant stopped serving, only a couple of reporters were still sitting doggedly over a pot of cold coffee. But when the waiters had finally persuaded them to leave, and went to clear the policeman's table, they discovered the following handwritten note concealed under a saucer: *'Thank you for a delightful meal. With compliments, MR BOLSOVER.'*

I am not sure how much credence to give to this account. Some of the details struck me as implaus-ible – for example, the restaurant was supposedly full, but why would so many people have turned out to see him when he was already a familiar figure in the town and, if the election result was anything to go by, a thoroughly unpopular one? A man who had once worked as a waiter at the Garden House told me categorically that Mr Bolsover had never eaten there, in disguise or out of it – apart from anything else, he said, he would have remembered the note, because they always used to pool their tips. But he was equally insistent that the incident had taken place, only at a different restaurant, the Golden Duck Chinese restaurant in the High Street, which has since closed down. I don't doubt that Mr Bolsover was capable of the exploit, but so many outlaws and fugitives before him have had similar adventures – 'Thou preparest a table before me in the presence of mine enemies,' as the psalm says – that I wonder whether it really happened.

Mr Bolsover himself, when questioned by Cooper, denied all these rumours. Starved of company, he had taken to dropping in at Barcombe Crescent when Cooper was cooking his evening meal, and they usually ended up eating together. He always brought a contribution to the meal – a salad of dandelion leaves, perhaps, or a handful of wild strawberries, slightly squashed from being in his pocket. When they finished eating he would follow Cooper out into the garden and watch with a critical eye as he weeded in between the rows of radishes. On wet nights he would push the empty plates aside and take a pack of grimy-edged cards from his pocket, and they would play rummy sitting there at the kitchen table. A strange kind of intimacy grew up between them, rather like that of an old married couple, where habit and routine take the place of conversation.

As a domestic arrangement it was perhaps unconventional, but such arrangements are not without precedent among high-minded visionary types. I think, for example, of Coleridge living with William Wordsworth and his sister Dorothy. The idea of an uncle sharing a house with his nephew seems quite straightforward by comparison.

But it would be wrong to suppose that their relations were entirely harmonious. When he moved into the house, Cooper had wiped away the dust that his uncle had allowed to collect on all the surfaces and cleaned the windows, and since then he had tried to keep the place reasonably tidy. But he was not prepared to take on the role of Dorothy Wordsworth, and now he found himself sweeping up his uncle's toast crumbs from the kitchen table, collecting the dirty plates and cups he left on top of the television, and straightening the sofa cushions. He soon became tired of his uncle's moods as well; he was often surly and snappish, like an old dog that lies in a corner and growls at anyone who comes near. There was also the matter of the hours that Mr Bolsover kept. By then he was largely nocturnal in his habits, and would happily continue their games of rummy well into the night, until Cooper was dizzy with fatigue, while his uncle only grew sharper and fresher with every hand they played.

What irked Cooper more than anything during this period was that his uncle showed no sign of wanting to change his situation. He made no further mention of any future plans, nor could he be drawn on the subject of the 'alternative measures' he had promised. He decided that Mr Bolsover either had no plan or, following his failure to join his uncle on Malling Hill, that he did have a plan but was no longer prepared to confide in him.

It was in this charged atmosphere that Cooper presented his uncle with a scheme for securing his return to office, this time as a member of Parliament. His motives in doing this were mixed. He hoped on one hand to prove himself, to regain his uncle's confidence, and on the other, in his own words, 'to bring the situation to a head'.

Over baked potatoes at a café in the High Street just down the hill from his office, Cooper outlined the scheme to me. It had been inspired, he told me, by his uncle's remark about redrawing the boundaries of his constituency.

'For an independent candidate,' he explained, 'there are certain challenges which the typical party hack doesn't face. How do you secure the votes you need to get elected when you don't have the backing of an organised party machine or the means to pay for billboards, TV advertising and that kind of thing? But then I had an idea: if we can't make sure of all those votes, why not take them out of the equation altogether?'

'I don't really follow.'

'Let me show you. Move those cups out of the way.' He took a map from his briefcase and opened it on the check tablecloth between us. 'These red lines represent the boundaries of the local parliamentary constituencies. From time to time, as I'm sure you know, these boundaries are adjusted to reflect changes in population, building developments and so forth. Now, my idea was to redraw the boundaries, creating an extra constituency here.' He took a pen from his pocket and traced a line round the edges of the wood.

'I know what you're thinking – what about the constituents?' He rummaged in his briefcase again and produced a piece of paper, which he unfolded on top of the map. 'This is the most recent survey by the Sussex Field Club of the bird population in these woods. You probably know there's a rookery at the northern end of the wood? Well, that rookery alone has over three thousand breeding pairs, or households as we'll call them for these purposes, and that's before you count the pigeons, the magpies and everything else.

'Then there's the dew pond in the corner here' – he circled it with his pen – 'which is positively teeming with frogs and newts. There must be several thousand tadpoles in there at the moment. Of course, as long as they remain tadpoles I think we have to regard them as minors. But once they've fully metamorphosed and emerged from the pond, it's a different story. It's true that a lot of them will then leave the constituency, but bearing in mind the life cycle of the common frog, and the fact that the elections are always held in May, I think it's reasonable to count them as resident when the time comes to vote.

'But the real population centre is the anthill. It's

not marked on the map, but it's just about here.' He tapped the map with the pen. 'Technically, I suppose it's a single household, but there should be fifty to seventy thousand adult individuals, and probably another ten thousand that are still pupating. There's also quite a large colony of badgers. I'm not sure what their domestic arrangements are, exactly – I can't very well get down a hole and count them – but let's say another five to ten households as a conservative estimate.

'Altogether that gives us an adult population of at least sixty thousand, and when you consider that there are sixty-eight thousand registered voters in the current Lewes constituency and sixty-six thousand in Brighton Kemptown, I think we have a fairly compelling case for the creation of a new constituency.'

'A rotten borough.'

'If you like.'

By this point in Cooper's recital I was feeling a growing sense of sympathy for his uncle. I began to think that Mr Bolsover had perhaps been right not to confide in him. Although at various moments during my conversations with him I had detected a tendency to embroider the facts, on this evidence Cooper was more of a fantasist than I had so far had occasion to suspect.

'But would the electoral committee have let you do something like that?' I asked.

'They didn't have to, because I wasn't going to consult them. It's just a matter of entering these population figures into the council's records and altering a few lines on the master copy of the constituency map.'

'How were you planning to do that?'

He gave me a faintly disappointed look. 'The details always fall into place when the time comes,' he said. 'I'm just outlining the strategy.'

'Won't they wonder why there's one more constituency than there was the last time they looked?'

'They probably won't notice. It's just a few more red lines on the map. And even if they do, so long as the population figures are there to back it up, no one's going to question it.'

'But even if you did manage to get sixty thousand assorted birds and frogs and ants onto the electoral register, they wouldn't exercise their right to vote, would they?'

'Obviously not,' Cooper said. 'But they don't have to. That's the whole point. I don't need them for that. I need electors who aren't going to exercise their right to vote. The number of active voters is very small. In fact, there's only one voter. And I cast my vote for the right candidate –'

'Just a minute – you're the voter, is that what you're saying?'

'That's right. Well, I don't know why you're looking so surprised,' he went on. 'Look where the boundary goes.'

The boundaries of the prospective rotten borough enclosed the wood and also the fields beyond it, as far as the western outskirts of Lewes. Halfway along this boundary, where the fields bordered Barcombe Crescent, there was a small salient as the boundary enclosed the perimeter of number seventeen. I reflected that this tract of unpopulated wood and grassland was Mr Bolsover's natural constituency, and that if he had been elected to represent an anthill and a pond full of frogspawn and a colony of badgers instead of the fractious and ungrateful voters of Winterbourne ward, he might have found his political career more fulfilling.

'Did you really think it would work?'

'I don't see why not.' There was a fanatical gleam in his eyes which unnerved me, and I think that if I had shown any interest he would have been perfectly happy for me to implement the proposal myself. It occurred to me that Cooper had spent so long in Mr Bolsover's company, had studied his example and preserved his memory so diligently, that he had to some extent metamorphosed into him. I saw him then not just as his uncle's amanuensis, but as his understudy. Throughout our conversation he had adopted the challenging tone familiar from Mr Bolsover's writings, and if I closed my eyes as he talked I could easily have believed that it was the man himself, and not his nephew, who was sitting across the table from me. And with his plans for the creation of a rotten borough, Cooper had conceived a scheme more ambitious, not to say more deranged, than anything his mentor might have attempted.

'What did your uncle think?'

Cooper's face darkened. 'He didn't like it.'

'What didn't he like about it?'

'He said it was impractical.'

'Really?' I found this reassuring.

'It wasn't so much his saying no that made me angry – of course he was entitled to refuse my help – but the fact that he called the plan impractical. Was it any more impractical than his election manifesto? He said he'd hoped I of all people would understand. I said I understood perfectly well – the way I saw it, he'd lost his nerve but he wasn't prepared to admit it.'

'What did he say to that?'

'He didn't say anything. He just got up and left.'

'Did you go after him?'

'No. It was nearly two in the morning. I locked the kitchen door and went to bed.'

When Cooper woke the next day and thought again about the night's events he had felt more kindly disposed towards his uncle. He wondered whether he had perhaps been too hard on him. But then he went downstairs and looked out of the kitchen window.

The vegetable bed, which had been a mass of luxuriant greenery the night before, was now a rectangle of churned and trampled earth. He pulled a coat on over his pyjamas and rushed outside to inspect the damage more closely. Everything had gone. The potatoes, radishes and beetroot had been grubbed up and their tops flung on the grass, the broad beans had been stripped from their stalks and the lettuces cut back to stumps. Even the leeks, which had only been in for a few weeks and were no bigger than spring onions, had all been torn from the ground. The garden fork was stuck in the earth in the middle of the bed, and impaled on one of its tines was a grubby piece of paper. Cooper tore it off and read it, although he had already guessed what would be written there: '*Mr Bolsover needs the vegetables.*'

It was not just the thoroughness of the destruction that shocked him, Cooper told me, but the proof it gave of Mr Bolsover's readiness to take ruthless and decisive action, to turn even against his oldest and most faithful lieutenant. But his own reaction was equally decisive. He went back into the house and called the police.

9

Operation Bedstraw

Cooper had been under no illusion that the wrecked vegetable bed was a police matter. But he knew his information about Mr Bolsover's cache of fireworks would be taken seriously, especially as the latest epidemic of exploding parking meters showed no sign of abating. The police had attended an incident at a car park that morning in which the charge had been placed for the first time underneath the machine, dislodging it from its foundations and cracking the paving slabs. This had been interpreted as an alarming escalation.

But these events on their own do not really account for the scale of the police response, or 'Operation Bedstraw', to give its official title, and I can only conclude that the feverish mood of rumour and conjecture about Mr Bolsover had affected even the police. The operation involved over a hundred officers from Sussex, Surrey and Kent, ten police dogs and their handlers from the Dog Section, a team of specialist firearms officers and the Air Support Unit.

Naturally enough, Cooper was not privy to the planning of the operation. The first he knew of it was when he received a call the night before, informing him that he would be needed to point out the exact location of Bolsover's bunker. He was to report to the car park behind the police station in North Street at four o'clock the next morning.

He set his alarm for half-past three, which would normally have given him plenty of time to get up and out of the house and across the town by four o'clock. So it may have been a measure of his ambivalent feelings about the whole enterprise that he did not arrive at the police station until five minutes past. In the floodlit car park, he found five police officers waiting by one of the vans that were parked on the tarmac. They were clutching polystyrene cups of tea and shuffling their feet to keep warm. Their sergeant came forward as Cooper approached, and introduced himself as the officer he had spoken to on the phone. The welcome was a little grudging, because Cooper was late.

They climbed into the back of the van. The sergeant started the engine and, conscious of being surrounded by policemen, Cooper fumbled to put his seatbelt on. The van drew up to the gates, which opened automatically, and they drove off through the empty streets in the bluish dawn light. The windows were soon misted over by the steam from the cups of tea. They headed out of Lewes in the direction of Brighton, and after they had gone about a mile down the road they pulled up in a lay-by in which, Cooper saw to his surprise, several police vehicles were already parked.

'Why are there so many vans?' he asked.

'It's not my decision,' the sergeant replied. 'It's the superintendent who's in charge of the operation.'

'But you did explain that he's just one person?'

'This man might seem harmless to you,' he said, 'but we have to think in terms of strategy. We don't know how he's going to react – people can become desperate when they're cornered. It's safer for everyone if we confront him right from the start with a show of overwhelming force. We probably won't have to use it.'

'How many people have you brought, altogether?' Cooper asked.

'You don't think we can mount a show of overwhelming force with five people, do you?' said the sergeant. 'Now come on, we'd better get moving. Everyone else will be in position by now.'

The policemen gathered round the back of the van,

grumbling and cursing under their breath as they unloaded their gear and put on their belts and stab vests. Meanwhile Cooper walked up and down the line of vehicles and counted three vans of a similar size to the one he had travelled in, a smaller van with a grille over the back window and 'Police Dogs' written on the side, and two patrol cars.

Returning to the van, he noticed that one officer had a shovel, and another was carrying a stout metal pole with handles a few inches from each end.

'What's that for?' Cooper asked.

'Breaking down doors.'

The sergeant slammed shut the doors of the van and they crossed the road and went through a gate and up a farm track, where they passed two private cars parked on the verge. 'Journalists,' said the sergeant. 'There's going to be a press conference later, but that's never enough for them. I hope they'll have the sense to keep out of the way.'

In the farmyard at the end of the track, a lorry marked 'Police Horses' was parked on the tarmac. 'In case he tries to make a break for it across country,' the sergeant explained. 'This is ideal terrain for a mounted pursuit. We probably won't need them, but it would be unforgivably negligent not to give ourselves the option.'

Leaving the farmyard, they followed a path that

climbed slowly up the long ridge behind the farm. As they approached the top of the ridge, Cooper saw a large group of police officers, also wearing helmets and stab vests, waiting just below the brow of the hill. He followed the sergeant to the top of the hill, while the others went to join their colleagues.

From here, looking down across the valley, with the wood filling the hollow and the bare hills rising all round, it was possible to get an idea of the scale of the operation. Cooper had never been up there so early in the morning: everything looked very still and peaceful, and birdsong rose from the wood, interspersed with the buzz and crackle of the police radios. It was cold too, and he began to shiver – he wished he had worn a warmer coat. In the distance he could see pairs of mounted police stationed on the hilltops above the wood, and as he watched a second group of officers on foot came over the ridge and down the hill and started to disperse round the far side of the wood. A short way down the slope to the right, a police marksman was moving into position in the lee of a thorn bush. He wore a peaked cap and carried a rifle with a telescopic sight, and he was signalling to a colleague on the hillside opposite.

'They're not going to shoot him, are they?'

'Only if he shoots first.'

'But he hasn't got a gun.'

'How do you know?' the sergeant said. 'He might have a concealed weapon. From your description we certainly expected him to be armed.'

'What do you mean, from my description?'

'A loner, grudge against society, hiding out in the woods, wanted on various charges – '

'That's not how I described him,' Cooper said indignantly.

'Those are the facts, though, aren't they?' said the sergeant. 'We can't take any risks with public safety, you know.'

He broke off for a brief and incomprehensible exchange over his radio, at the end of which he turned to Cooper and said, 'We're ready to go.' The group of officers behind them began to disperse. Some fanned out along the edges of the wood, while the others followed Cooper and the sergeant down to the track leading into the wood, where several police dogs and their handlers were waiting. As they went down the hill the air was rent by the noise of a helicopter labouring overhead and lowering itself slowly above the trees with a massive drumming of its engine.

The sergeant gave his final briefing. They were to divide into two groups. Cooper would lead one group directly to the bunker, while the other group, including the dogs, would bring up the rear, moving through the wood in a line abreast in case Mr Bolsover tried to slip past them in the undergrowth.

The sergeant's instructions were simple enough, but Cooper could barely take them in. He was conscious of a sinking feeling, which grew stronger as he went up the track and into the wood accompanied by the sergeant and several officers. Although he had set the whole operation in motion, it had been painfully clear to him ever since his arrival at the police station that morning that he was caught up in a situation that was beyond his control, and as the inevitable confrontation with Mr Bolsover drew closer he found the tension increasingly difficult to bear. The policemen spread out in a line behind him, then left the track and went up the slope through the hazel coppice, kicking through last year's dead leaves. From above the trees came the ominous sound of the helicopter churning the air as it bore down on them, and Cooper began to have deep misgivings about the whole undertaking. He had an urge to lead them in the wrong direction, or to run off between the trees and lose them altogether. But he knew already that it was too late for that.

'Don't get too far ahead,' called the officer with the battering ram. 'I don't want to be wandering about in the woods all day with this thing.' Cooper looked back, and saw that in his reverie he had left the line of police some way behind him. He stopped to let them catch up and as they came on, crashing through the undergrowth, stamping on twigs and kicking up the leaves, he thought how his uncle would scoff at the noise they were making.

They passed the familiar landmarks: the badgers' setts, the oak tree with ferns growing on its branches, and finally the holly bush flanked by two ash trees. Here Cooper stopped and looked cautiously down on the hollow where Mr Bolsover had dug himself in.

'Is this the place, then?' asked the sergeant, when they were all standing together on the edge of the hollow. 'Where's the dugout?' Cooper pointed out the tree roots and the trailing ivy that concealed the entrance to the bunker.

'You'd better stay here for now,' the sergeant told Cooper. 'We don't want you getting in the way.' They stood together under the dripping branches while the others scrambled down into the hollow. Four took up positions a short distance from the dugout while the rest, equipped with shovels and the battering ram, went up to the entrance, put down their tools and began to tear away the curtain of ivy. Watching them, Cooper was put in mind of a badger being dug out of its sett.

One officer crouched down and knocked on the door of the bunker, and Cooper was just thinking that this observation of domestic niceties in the middle of the woods was rather absurd, when somebody shouted, 'Armed police!' The four officers standing back from the entrance had snatched their pistols from their belts and were covering their colleague while he banged again on the door. Cooper watched anxiously as he tried the handle of the door, then rattled it.

'It's probably stuck,' Cooper said to the sergeant. 'When the weather's damp like this it usually gets stuck, you just have to give it a shove.' But they had already brought up the battering ram: a couple of blows and the door came off its hinges. They shone their flashlights into the bunker, examining it the way a dentist peers into the recesses of a patient's mouth, then signalled to the others that there was no one inside.

The officers covering them lowered their guns and Cooper had no sense of anticlimax or disappointment, only an overwhelming feeling of relief. Approaching the dugout he had imagined the moment when the fugitive would be dragged from his lair, and pictured with horrible clarity the accusatory look on Mr Bolsover's face when he recognised his nephew among his captors. Now it seemed that they would both be spared the confrontation.

But his relief did not last long. The policemen who had broken down the door lost no time in pushing their way into the dugout: Cooper hurried across the clearing, and was soon watching guiltily from the doorway as they examined all the objects on the shelves, holding them under their flashlights, and knocking over Mr Bolsover's tooth mug in the process. They kneaded the cushions and then leafed methodically through the pages of his books, dislodging a number of pressed flowers, which they retrieved from the floor and sealed in plastic bags for forensic examination.

The bed had been slept in: the blankets were rumpled and the pillow dented. The sergeant put his hand on the sheet and invited Cooper to do the same. The bedclothes were still warm. Burrowing further, they discovered the fugitive's hot-water bottle.

'He was here last night, then,' Cooper said, as they crawled out into the daylight again.

'Clearly,' said the sergeant. 'Now, what about that cache of explosives?'

Cooper led them over to Mr Bolsover's root cellar and watched as they pulled the ivy away and shone their torches inside. The rockets had gone, and in their place lay a small packet of sparklers. The sergeant looked grave.

'He must have heard us arriving,' Cooper said.

'More likely he knew we were coming,' said the sergeant. 'Somebody must have tipped him off.'

They all looked at Cooper darkly, and it dawned on him that he was their chief suspect. But it made no sense: why would he report Mr Bolsover to the police and then warn him they were coming? Perhaps they reasoned that if he was capable of one act of treachery in betraying his uncle, he was capable of another.

Before Cooper could answer, a noise of shouting and dogs barking came from the edge of the wood away to the right. The rooks cawed in alarm and the radios began to chatter excitedly. 'They've apprehended some-one,' the sergeant said. 'We may need you to identify him. Come with me.'

He hurried away through the trees in the direction of the noise, leaving his colleagues to finish examin-ing the bunker and taking photographs. With a heavy heart, Cooper followed. So the reckoning had not been avoided, only postponed, and the saga would end here, with Mr Bolsover flushed from cover like a hunted ani-mal and run down by dogs on a lonely hillside. This was what he had dreaded: coming face to face with his uncle in circumstances where there could be no concealing the fact of his betrayal. But he was resigned to it now. He had cast himself in this part and now, he reflected mournfully, he must be prepared to play it.

Emerging at last from the wood, he saw the sergeant standing in the field with a group of half a dozen or so police officers who were arguing with a disgruntled-looking man in a torn raincoat. For the second time that morning, he felt a great surge of relief: it was not Mr Bolsover. Seeing Cooper, the sergeant detached himself from the group and came over.

'False alarm,' he said. 'Turns out he's a journalist. He must have got here before we did, and he was hiding just down there – I suppose he thought he might see something. But the dogs smelt him as they came through. He must be quite a runner – he was halfway up the hill before they caught him. He's cross now, of course,' he added, 'but frankly he was very lucky not to be shot.'

They waited there until the line of police and dogs had worked its way through to the end of the wood. But there was still no trace of the fugitive, and in time the search was abandoned. The helicopter rose into the sky and flew away, and the mounted police and marksmen left their hilltop positions. As they gathered at the entrance to the wood before returning to the vans the mood was sombre and Cooper understood, from odd looks and muttered comments, that the sergeant was not the only one who suspected him of warning Mr Bolsover about Operation Bedstraw. In fact the atmosphere was distinctly uncomfortable, and he decided not to return to Lewes in the police van but to walk home on his own across the downs.

He followed the footpath up the hillside, and as he climbed higher his spirits began to rise. The sun was up, and he felt its warmth on his face. At the top of the hill he turned and looked round. Below him he could see the last of the police officers returning in straggling groups down the track to where their vehicles were parked, and the wood, in its wide shallow valley, appeared peaceful and deserted once more. He walked on across the dewy grass towards the town, feeling as though he had been granted a reprieve.

10

The Making of Mr Bolsover

Later that day a press conference was held in a crowded, stuffy little room in the police station. It had been scheduled for eleven o'clock but did not start until one. The official explanation for this delay was the need to deal with administrative matters arising from the operation that morning, but the more cynical members of the press corps assumed that it had been deliberately engineered in the hope that they would get tired of waiting and go away.

The police had been anticipating a triumph. They had hoped to announce the arrest of Mr Bolsover and to regale an admiring audience with the details of their meticulously planned and brilliantly executed operation to capture him. Instead, they found themselves facing a group of journalists rendered more than usually hostile and combative by what had happened to their colleague

– they had all seen what the dogs had done to his rain-coat and his trouser cuffs – and by the delayed start to the proceedings.

The superintendent did his best. The search for Mr Bolsover, he said, was 'still ongoing'. A number of items had been recovered from his bunker which might provide clues to his whereabouts and they were now being examined by a forensics team. Meanwhile, the sergeant said, Interpol had been alerted, and a close watch was being kept on the ferry ports at Newhaven and Dover and on Gatwick Airport in case he attempted to flee the country.

But the journalists would have none of it. Cooper stood at the back of the room and watched as the two policemen grew haggard and miserable under the barrage of questions. Did Bolsover still present a danger to the public? Did the superintendent attribute the failure of the operation to his own poor leadership, the low calibre of the officers under his command, or a combination of the two? Did he intend to resign? At last, when the details of the operation had been picked over to the journalists' satisfaction and examined from every conceivable unflattering angle, the press conference drew to a close.

The journalists had been so concerned with what had happened to their colleague and with the shortcomings of the police that they had failed to address the questions of how Mr Bolsover had escaped and where he had gone. The bolt-holes, the new tunnels he had boasted of to Cooper – did they exist after all? Had he made his escape through one of them, or simply slipped through the police lines as they closed in? Was he still at large in the woods, only deeper underground, in a bunker whose existence and location was unknown even to Cooper? Had he left for another town, to begin a new life under a different name? Or was he already on his way to New South Wales in search of his wife, hoping to win back her love in some secluded valley of the Blue Mountains, in the shade of the ghost gums?

These questions preoccupied Cooper all afternoon, and when he got home that evening he was still pondering them as he tidied the wrecked vegetable bed. By the time he came to put the tools away the light was beginning to fade. A bat flitted over his head and disappeared behind the lilac bushes, and he looked up just in time to see a rocket shooting into the sky behind the hill and exploding. Cooper stood still. It was – it could only be – Mr Bolsover's private signal! He ran to the shed to fetch one of his own rockets, but haste and nerves made his hands unsteady and no sooner had he stuck it in the earth and lit the fuse than it keeled over and streaked off on a dangerously low trajectory, bursting above the garden of number forty-three. Ashamed of his clumsiness, he hurried out of the gate and up over the hill.

The hedges and thorn bushes cast long shadows across the fields and as he came down the slope towards the wood he saw nobody at the stile. He waited for a minute or two and called out several times, but there was no answer. At last he climbed over the stile and went on into the wood. It was almost dark under the trees and he could barely make out the path in front of him. When he reached the site of Mr Bolsover's camp it had been cordoned off, with ribbons of police tape stretched between the trees and looped round their trunks. During the day they must have brought an earth mover to knock in the roof and fill the dugout with soil, because the clearing had been churned up by caterpillar tracks and the bunker covered with a pile of loose earth, like a freshly filled-in grave. Looking at it Cooper felt a pang, as if his uncle really had been buried under there.

As he went closer, ducking under the police tape, he noticed that someone had stuck a twig in the top of the mound, like a grave-marker. The twig was split down the middle, and wedged into it was a piece of folded paper. Intrigued, he picked the paper out and unfolded it. Scrawled on it in pencil, in capital letters, in Bolsover's handwriting, were the words '*I SHALL RETURN*'.

Cooper's heart began to pound and he looked wildly about him in the darkening wood, peering into the shadows, alert for any sign of movement. A jay shrieked in the branches above his head, and in a panic he flung himself against the nearest tree, stuffing the note into his trouser pocket. The feel of the rough bark against his back calmed him a little, and as the minutes went by he finally concluded that he was alone in the wood after all, or at least that if Mr Bolsover was there, he was not about to show himself. He decided to retrace his steps and go home before the light failed completely.

Later that night Cooper was in the kitchen when he heard a noise outside. With some trepidation he went to open the door, but there was nobody there. It was only the hedgehog, nosing at the empty saucer by the boot-scraper and looking up at him with its beady black eyes. And it was at that moment, Cooper told me afterwards, that he understood the significance of his uncle's note. He was not consoled, exactly – after all, it was as much a threat as a promise. But with it, he felt, Mr Bolsover had passed from this world and into the realm of myth. Wherever he was now, in Crawley or Cabramatta, or sleeping in a cavern under the chalk hills with his hand on his sword, there was no point in looking for him any further. One might as well mount a search for King Arthur.

He went back into the kitchen to open a tin of cat food and scooped some out onto the saucer. For such a small creature the hedgehog made a surprising amount of noise as it ate, bumping the saucer and making it scrape and rattle on the concrete. When the saucer was empty it turned its back and crept away into the darkness. Cooper shut the door and went to bed.

Next day he woke with a sore throat and a temperature: he guessed he had caught a cold getting up so early and standing about in the woods with the police. He went into work all the same, but during the morning he started to feel feverish and short of breath, and at lunchtime the editor told him to go home. His symptoms developed into a chest infection, and he had to spend several days in bed.

But the curious thing was that even after he had recovered and gone back to work he continued to suffer intermittently from shortness of breath. He would find himself wheezing as he climbed the stairs, or when he sat down at his desk in the mornings. After a few weeks of this he went to see a doctor, who examined him and said that he probably had mild asthma. This diagnosis struck Cooper as highly significant; after all, his uncle had suffered from asthma.

'Have you ever come across a case of asthma being transferred from one person to another?' he asked.

'It's not infectious, if that's what you mean,' the doctor told him.

'Not exactly,' Cooper said. 'I mean, my uncle had asthma, and now I've got it.'

'That's quite likely,' she said, 'it often runs in families.'

But that was not it either. What Cooper believed was that his uncle's asthma had communicated itself to him. I don't know whether this is medically possible: frankly I doubt it, and I was not surprised to hear that he had not questioned the doctor any further on the subject. It was fairly clear to me that he had yielded to the temptation that faces anyone who encounters a figure of Mr Bolsover's stature, to exaggerate and mythologise their dealings with him. They try to glorify themselves by association and also perhaps to compensate, because measured against his magnificent trajectory they see how mundane, how shadowy and insubstantial their own lives have been in comparison.

But perhaps I am being unfair to Cooper, who was recently appointed assistant news editor on the *Brighton Echo*. He had some reason to think of himself as the keeper of his uncle's flame: he continued to live at Barcombe Crescent, and the standing order for his rent still went out at the end of each month. He had no way of knowing whether the money was being spent, he said, or piling up untouched in his uncle's account, but he felt that as long as he lived in the house he should go on paying the rent. Perhaps too he saw the payments as a way of atoning for his earlier betrayal, whether as contributions to a cause, like his subscription to the Wildlife Trust, or as tribute, like the Danegeld, paid by fearful Saxons in the Dark Ages to keep the barbarian from the gates.

In any case, Cooper was not alone in his myth-making. At times the whole of Lewes was at it. After Mr Bolsover disappeared there was an extraordinary flowering of rumour and speculation about him, verging on collective hysteria. When, for example, the railway line between Lewes and Newhaven was closed one weekend for emergency engineering work, it was said that the track had been mined by the partisans (for Mr Bolsover soon became in myth what he had never been in reality, the leader of a shadowy fighting force), and that illegal barricades were being set up after dark on the country roads. There were reports of strange flickering lights observed at night in the woods above Offham, while a grainy photograph circulated on internet forums purportedly showing a final ultimatum from Mr Bolsover found pinned with a dagger to the door of the council chamber. And I met one of his former neighbours, a retired inspector of schools, who lived across the road from him at Barcombe Crescent and struck me as a sober and respectable member of the community, but claimed nevertheless to have seen Mr Bolsover snooping round her henhouse one evening. When I asked her to describe him, she said he had been naked except for a belt with a pistol at his waist, a dense coat of curly hair all over his body, and terrible burning eyes that shone red in the light of her torch.

Mr Bolsover's earthworks also exercised a strange fascination. His foxhole, as the police had described it at the press conference, grew in size each time it was discussed. Initially a mere scraping in the ground, very soon it was being spoken of as a vast network of tunnels and chambers which extended beneath the town centre itself, undermining the foundations of the banks and the public buildings. I was assured by more than one employee of the Borough Council that a secret passage led from Mr Bolsover's bunker in the woods directly to the council offices, emerging in the washroom next to the council chamber. A resident of Meridian Road told me that half the houses in his street had been pronounced structurally unsound by a surveyor, and that in the last six months alone the spire of St Michael's Church had listed four inches off the vertical at its apex.

At the primary school in De Montfort Road the care-taker showed me several large cracks in the playground which he said had recently appeared and which were, in his words, 'big enough to swallow a dog'. In the King's Head one night they told me that the western end of the High Street was showing signs of subsidence, and within a few years entire buildings might collapse into Mr Bolsover's subterranean workings. Other more hysterical voices insisted that the tunnels had been packed with explosives, and that if he chose to Mr Bolsover could blow the whole town to pieces simply by dropping a lighted match between the bars of a certain drain cover outside the bus station.

Listening to these reports, I began to fear not so much for the physical stability of the town as for the mental stability of its inhabitants.

It is customary to end a political biography with an appraisal of the subject's achievements. Although Mr Bolsover made an indelible impression on everyone who met him, and on many who did not, he left little in the way of a political legacy in the conventional sense. No new initiatives were adopted as a result of his actions, and he could not boast, as councillors from the other parties liked to do at election time, of securing funds from central government for the renovation of school buildings, or holding social care service providers to account, or improving road safety, or freezing council tax.

But to judge him a failure on those grounds would be to misunderstand him, as I believe Cooper ultimately misunderstood him. If his career was not a success in conventional terms, perhaps he never intended it to be. It is always possible that the whole of his time in office – the meetings, the surgeries, the machinations in smoke-free council corridors – was only a preparatory stage, and that the voters' rejection of Mr Bolsover's appeal to them marked not the end of his political career but the beginning of a new phase. I know that for the biographer this is dangerous ground: I am moving from the realm of fact to the realm of conjecture. But with a subject who began as a man and ended as a myth it is hard to do otherwise, and I can only extrapolate from what I know of his character.

'The most significant feature in the history of an epoch,' writes Carlyle, 'is the manner it has of welcoming a Great Man.' I am convinced that Mr Bolsover was a member of that rare species, which has so often been pronounced extinct, and it strikes me that the manner of his welcome does the present epoch little credit. But I cannot believe that he simply became a fugitive. A greater destiny surely awaited him: to maintain his private republic in that redoubt on the upper slopes of the downs, alongside those other rare creatures, the glow-worms and the dormice and the Roman snails. And I feel entitled to believe, at least until I see evidence to the contrary, that somewhere in the woods Mr Bolsover's campaign continues.

Acknowledgements

Thank you to Charles Collier, Stuart Williams, Matthew Dixon and Simon Rhodes.

I consulted various biographies and other works while writing this book. Some are mentioned in the text. I would like to acknowledge several which are not, namely Roy Jenkins' *Askwith* (1978), *Baldwin* (1984), *Gladstone* (1995) and *Churchill* (2001), Robert Taylor's *Lord Salisbury* (1975) and Gordon Campbell's *The Hermit in the Garden* (2013).